War Games

a novel based on a true story

Newbery Honor Winner
AUDREY COULOUMBIS
& AKILA COULOUMBIS

RANDOM HOUSE
NEW YORK

Published in the United States by Random House Children's Books,
a division of Random House, Inc., New York.

Random House and the colophon are registered trademarks of Random House, Inc.

Visit us on the Web!
www.randomhouse.com/kids

Educators and librarians, for a variety of teaching tools,
visit us at www.randomhouse.com/teachers

Library of Congress Cataloging-in-Publication Data
Couloumbis, Audrey.
War games / by Audrey and Akila Couloumbis. — 1st ed.
p. cm.
"Based on a true story."
Summary: What were once just boys' games become matters of life and death as
Petros and his older brother Zola each wonder if, like their resistance fighter
cousin, they too can make a difference in a Nazi-occupied Greece.
ISBN 978-0-375-85628-0 (trade) — ISBN 978-0-375-95628-7 (lib. bdg.) —
ISBN 978-0-375-89302-5 (e-book)
1. World War, 1939 1945—Underground movements—Greece—Juvenile fiction.
2. Greece—History—Occupation, 1941–1944—Juvenile fiction.
[1. World War, 1939–1945—Underground movements—Greece—Fiction.
2. Greece—History—Occupation, 1941–1944—Fiction. 3. Brothers—Fiction.
4. Cousins—Fiction.] I. Couloumbis, Akila. II. Title.
PZ7.C8305War 2009
[Fic]—dc22
2008046784

Printed in the United States of America

10 9 8 7 6 5 4 3 2 1

First Edition

I dedicate my contribution to this book
to Aspasia and Peter, the heroes of my youth,
and to my wife and children,
who've become my heroes
since they came into my life.

—Akila

To Mama Nicky's children.

—Audrey

chapter 1

"I can hit the next three birds we see," Zola said.

Petros shrugged. His older brother liked to make a contest of things.

They sat on a rock wall in the cooling green shade of the arbor, each with a small pile of stones beside his right hand. Above them, the weight of the grapevines rested on thick beams, the leaves trembling with the activity of so many small birds they could not be counted.

Zola made a confident sound with his breath and said again, "I can shoot three birds without missing."

"Maybe you can," Petros said, in a way that meant *and maybe you can't*. Zola had just turned fifteen the day before Easter, making this the first of several unbearable months during which he would be three years older than Petros, instead of only two.

"If I do," Zola said, "you do my chores for three days."

A week ago, Zola made a parachute for his little white dog, using a basket and a small tablecloth. Petros told his brother it was a stupid idea. The dog would have nothing to do with it either.

Still determined, Zola had carried their sister's rickety old cat up to the flat rooftop, where there was always a strong breeze. He put the cat in the basket and threw her off the house. The parachute worked. If the basket didn't precisely float to the ground, it didn't fall fast.

Best, it landed in a bush and the cat wasn't hurt.

Worst, the basket landed in the bush in front of the window where Mama stood, looking out. Zola's chores were doubled to keep him busy. Also, the cat scratched him. Stupid idea.

Now Petros scooped up a few stones and let them fall, *tik, tik, tik.* "Three days is too many."

"Three birds." Zola poked him with an elbow. "Three in a row."

Petros wanted to poke him back but didn't. "If you can do it, I can do it."

"Then why haven't you?" Zola asked.

"I never thought of it, that's why." If ever he had another choice of big brother, Petros decided, he would pick one less irritating.

Zola held his slingshot straight out and pulled back on the stone. He waited, his eyes searching for a target. The doves were big and slow. But they were Mama's. She'd be angry if her birds got hurt.

They didn't like to hit the many-colored finches, their favorites. And Zola dared not hit a swallow. A red blotch at the swallows' throats was said to be a drop of the blood of Christ.

Extremely bad luck came to anyone who hurt one of these birds.

That left only one worthy target. Sparrows were sharp-eyed and smart, and therefore nervous. Small and fast, they were hard to hit.

A bird moved through the tangle of vines. Zola let his stone fly, shooting through a space between the leaves. The bird dropped to the ground without a flutter.

"A lucky shot," Petros said.

"An excellent shot," Zola said, setting another stone.

"Excellent luck," Petros argued. To send a stone through the knotted vines could be nothing else. Even so, Petros admired the shot.

Zola said, "I could do it again if a bird would land there." Petros rolled his eyes. Of all the older brothers he knew, Zola was the worst.

A sparrow touched down where a vine hung below the arbor. The bird fell without waking Zola's dog, only a few feet away. An ordinary shot, and Zola didn't brag.

Again, the wait, watching. A careless target landed on a branch nearby. Zola got his third bird. "Ya-ha," he shouted. "Three days!"

"No," Petros said. "That was your bet. Here's mine: I'll kill two birds with one stone. Then you'll do my chores."

"For one morning," Zola said agreeably.

"Three."

"Two."

"Three." Petros felt in his pocket for a piece of shiny white marble, freckled with purple dots. Lucky, he thought, but he hadn't tried it yet. As with all things lucky, the right time would come.

"Perhaps we'll strike a bargain," Zola said. "Right now you owe me three days."

"I owe you nothing," Petros said, "but two dead birds."

He held out his lucky stone, easy to spot if it fell to the ground under the arbor. A blackbird landed in the garden outside the grape arbor and plucked a tiny beet plant. Petros set the stone into his slingshot and let it fly. The eager gardener fell over.

Petros ran over and picked up the stone. At the same time, their sister's cat made a labored dash from a hiding place beneath the arbor to steal the blackbird.

The dash was more a matter of pride than necessity. The bird was too dead to put up a fight, the cat so aged she could hardly catch anything on her own. When the boys hunted, the cat ate.

As Petros turned, he saw a sparrow land on the grapevine above Zola. He aimed and, seeing the challenge on Zola's face, shot. The stone nicked a stem on the branch the bird sat upon, cutting off a twig with two leaves that fell right on Zola's head.

"Ha!" Zola cried.

"I can try again," Petros said.

"No, you can't," Zola said. "It had to be two birds in a row."

"I can do it, you know." Petros had shot two birds in a row before.

Zola grinned. Switching from English to Greek, he said, "Here comes Stavros. Hit *that* bird and you don't have to do my chores."

Their cousin walked the mile from the village of Amphissa once or twice a week. He saw them in the shadows and pulled his own slingshot from his pocket.

"Don't tease him," Petros said.

Zola shrugged. Then he started trouble with his next breath. "I hit three birds in a row," he said, "and Petros could not."

"I said I would hit two birds with one stone." The rock with purple spots hadn't been so lucky after all, but it was still interesting.

Stavros leaned in to Petros and said out of the corner of his mouth, "Perhaps Zola was just lucky."

"I can do it again anytime," Zola said. "I can do it now."

"So do it," Stavros said, daring him.

"You do it first," Zola said. "If you can't, why should I bother?"

Stavros let his brows lower to cover his eyes like a shelf. Zola wouldn't let Stavros win and Stavros couldn't bear to lose. "Never mind," Petros said to them. "We've scared away the birds."

Zola said, "I have something else to do anyway."

Petros wanted to kick Zola. It was just like his brother to

make Stavros mad and then leave Petros to smooth the ruffled feathers. He hoped Zola hadn't ruined Stavros for the day.

Suddenly, Stavros shot into the nearby olive tree. A bird fell to the ground at Zola's feet. Petros stared at the small bird's lifeless form, at the small spot of red feathers at its throat.

"Are you crazy?" Zola shouted. "You killed a swallow." Zola's dog lifted his head at the sound of trouble.

Stavros quivered with anger. "I can shoot three of them."

Zola threw his slingshot down. "This is what I get for playing with little boys." He walked away, his dog following like a pale shadow.

Petros could think of only one thing to do. He told Stavros, "If we give the swallow a burial, the cat won't get it."

Together, he and Stavros dug a hole for the swallow.

Even though Petros had been born half a world away, he'd known his cousin for as long as he could remember. They'd shared as many games and fights as any brothers. Petros was worried about the bad luck that would follow Stavros now.

"Maybe you should say you're sorry," he suggested as they scooped dirt over the body.

"It was an accident."

Petros nodded. In twelve years, he'd often wished for a cousin with a little less iron in his spine. This was as close to an apology as he'd ever heard Stavros come.

chapter 2

When Petros rose at sunup three days later, his first thought made him grin. Today Zola had to take back his chores. No more early-morning milking of goats for Petros, and so no kicks and bites and bruises.

Also, more sleep.

No scrubbing the small pots used for starting seeds. No shoveling rotting leaves and chopped-up stalks from one smelly compost heap to the next.

He carried his breakfast of polenta with raisins outside, where he sat on the steps at the kitchen door. In ten minutes he'd be feeding the pig and Mama's chickens, but after three days of Zola lording the wager over him, the day felt like a holiday.

While he ate, he noticed the first tightly wrapped artichokes growing near the house. Papa called this counting his money. He meant this was how he earned the drachmas he put in the box under his bed.

Lately all Greeks were poor. Petros didn't understand why, but the surrender to the Germans meant the drachma was now worthless. People had begun to trade, rather than to buy and sell.

Mama traded seeds for more chickens. Petros hoped the plants from his garden would yield good seeds.

Zola was raking the goats' pen, keeping up a steady stream of curses. The eldest nanny goat nipped him on the arm. "Yow! Get away!" Another butted him from behind. Petros grinned. Three days only and Zola was no longer a match for these goats.

Petros looked for his favorite and saw the little black goat digging a hole at the back of the shed. He stayed a little separate from the rest.

After feeding the pig and chickens, Petros went to a pile of stones Zola had left for him at the end of the low wall they were building. Over some weeks, Zola had cleared a piece of land, digging up enough stones for Petros to build this low wall along one side of the garden. He drove a stick into the dirt where he'd left off the day before. He measured his progress in strides.

When Papa came along and sat on the wall, Petros had already set enough new stones to pass them with five strides. Papa nodded—the wall was good—and then said, "We're fortunate to have these baby goats."

Three kids were born on Easter day, a late litter, but these were Silky's babies and so were no surprise. Silky was late in everything, even to meals.

The smallest and most sweet-natured of these kids, born

last, was black. Papa dubbed him "a lump of coal" at first sight. Male goats didn't make milk, they became stew meat. Petros kept quiet, afraid for Lump.

"It's bad luck two of the babies were male," Papa added.

This Easter there were German air raids over Greece. For their family it was windows broken and chickens killed. Many other families weren't so lucky. The village held several funerals. Nothing of that day was considered to be good luck.

"My brother Spiro's goat gave birth to females," Papa said.

Uncle Spiro lived farther away from Amphissa, perhaps two miles from town. Papa and Uncle Spiro hadn't spoken to each other in years. No one remembered why. Anything one of them wanted to say to the other was passed along by someone else. Petros hoped he was about to carry one of these messages.

Papa said, "I propose we trade him one of our male goats for one of his. He won't have to sacrifice a female for meat."

Petros's heart immediately felt lighter. "Good idea, Papa," he said. His uncle Spiro ate very little meat because, he sometimes said, he had no wife to cook it. Lump would be safe there.

"You'll take the white and tell him of this plan. Perhaps he'll agree."

Petros's heart fell. "Or I could take Lump," he suggested.

"Take the best," Papa said. "I can offer nothing less."

He left Petros, having set down his plan.

Petros understood offering the larger goat. But the small

black goat would then land in Mama's stew pot. Pulling his shoulders back so he would feel tall, Petros tied a rope around the neck of the black kid.

They stood in the shadow of the goat shed until Papa had pushed a wheelbarrow to the far end of the garden. Petros tried to look innocent as he led the little goat away.

Old Mario, the hired hand, worked in the garden. He wore a straw hat and a shirt with soft, loose sleeves. The air shifted around him in wavy lines, hot and dry. He didn't notice Petros.

But as Petros approached the gate, Zola came from the orchard. "That isn't the goat Papa meant for you to take."

"I know it." Petros walked faster.

Zola said, "Papa's going to be mad."

Petros hurried along the dusty road to Uncle Spiro's farm, Lump trailing behind. He'd hoped to feel brave and bold once he'd left the farmyard, but the knot in his stomach kept reminding him he was neither.

He'd walked halfway to his uncle's, mostly uphill under the hot sun, without noticing, before he passed some Italian soldiers who took his mind off this trouble. One of them waved to him, smiling. Petros didn't wave back.

He'd once watched Italian soldiers steal tomatoes from their garden. Papa allowed this. The soldiers carried guns. Papa put a heavy chain on the gate only minutes after the soldiers walked away. But he let the soldiers take the tomatoes.

Since last year, 1940, the small Greek army had been fighting the Italians back into Albania man against man. Greece won the battles in the air with only their old biplanes, shooting down newer, faster planes.

For many pleasant evenings, Petros listened to reports of these battles on the radio along with his friend Elia—with the whole Lemos family gathered in Mama's parlor.

But when the Germans sent troops through Bulgaria, the Greek army rushed to defend another border. The Italian soldiers streamed through the undefended mountain passes. Now they camped around the countryside, living an uneasy truce.

Sometimes the soldiers charmed a lonely old person into sharing a meal with them. Otherwise they cooked tomatoes over their fires and said their prayers on Sunday. The wily ones also stole chickens.

If he were a full-grown man, Petros thought, he wouldn't be afraid. Among Mama and her friends, there was talk of chasing the Italian army back to Italy. Petros suspected the women could do it. The soldiers looked no older than Zola.

They'd rolled their jackets to make pillows and dropped their guns in the sparse grass of the rocky hillside. Smoking and talking, they laughed over a joke. One of them called out to Petros.

"Do you want to sell that goat?" This was the kind of trouble these soldiers gave people. Always hungry. And now that they'd begun speaking Greek, they liked to tease.

"This goat is my sister's favorite," Petros said, pulling Lump along a little faster. He'd have said Lump was his favorite, but these soldiers often had a soft spot in their hearts for sisters.

"What has she named it, this favorite?"

Because Sophie had named *her* favorite, Petros said, "Pearl."

The soldiers laughed. They offered Petros a piece of soft white candy with fruit and nuts. He hated to turn it down, but he shook his head, never stopping. If the soldiers stole Lump, the little goat would be in a stew pot before the day was out.

Passing them, he asked, "When are the Germans coming?"

"Why would they come?" one soldier replied. "We're here already."

"Everyone is afraid the Germans are coming," Petros said.

"A strategy," another soldier said. "While you're talking, you're not fighting, isn't it so?" A few of the soldiers laughed, and Petros hurried on his way, glad little Lump hadn't looked more appetizing.

chapter 3

Uncle Spiro's farm had a stream and many old olive trees. But the house needed a coat of paint. The chicken house needed repairs. And the garden always needed weeding.

The reason for this was simple. Uncle Spiro sang and even danced as he worked. He preferred to lay down the work for the dancing, and often did. Zola once said this was because he was a younger brother, and Papa appeared to agree.

Petros found him at an old table under the grape arbor.

"Hello, Petros," Uncle Spiro called out.

"You'll like it here, little Lump," Petros told the kid when it balked.

His uncle's breakfast of hard bread and strong coffee sat neglected as he adjusted the strings on his guitar. "Uncle," Petros said, "could I trade this male for one of your females?"

"Excellent idea." Uncle Spiro pointed out his largest kid.

"Papa told me to bring you our biggest one. But I've brought you the smallest."

"He's captured your heart," Uncle Spiro said.

Petros wasn't ashamed to admit it. "He's good-natured for a goat."

"Then you must take Fifi." Uncle Spiro pointed to a white goat grazing some distance away. A rope tied around her neck dragged on the ground, as if she'd been waiting for someone to take her away.

"She isn't the largest, but she isn't the smallest either. She'll give milk and she'll have many babies to give more milk. And"—Uncle Spiro raised a hand so one finger pointed to the sky, his way of saying this would be the important part—"you'll tell your papa you made a fine bargain and we're both content."

"Papa will be angry anyway."

Uncle Spiro laughed. "Not when he comes to know Fifi. She bites hard, and I swear to you, she spits like a camel. I don't prefer her, and your papa, he won't like her either. He'll congratulate you for giving up only the small goat."

"Small, but sweet." Petros patted the hard bump of Lump's head.

"Sturdy, too," Uncle Spiro said, wrapping his hand around Lump's ankle. "He'll grow. Perhaps he'll be the biggest of all."

Petros noticed there were two cups of coffee poured. "Uncle, are you waiting for someone?"

"No, no," he said, picking out a little tune on his guitar.

Zola had recently whispered to Petros that their uncle was rumored to have hidden some British soldiers from the Italians. Petros didn't believe it. Their uncle was not the serious type.

They sang songs until, at home, the family would think of

eating lunch. Petros wasn't in a hurry. After the meal, the family would find places to sit or sleep quietly through the afternoon heat. Only when the air cooled a little would the work begin again.

"We've surrendered in Salonika," Uncle Spiro said, naming the town in northern Greece. "What are people saying in our village?"

"That the Germans will come soon. Somebody paints Greek flags on the sides of buildings," Petros said. "And words."

"Words. Against the Germans?"

Petros nodded. "Some people hang small flags from their windows or chimneys for everyone to see. But whoever paints the words, they do it at night, when no one will see them."

Uncle Spiro made a tight little circle of his lips, thinking.

"Mama won't send us to school," Petros said. "Everyone waits. I thought Papa always knew what to do. But now—"

"He plants another row. He picks another crop," Uncle Spiro said. "It's enough for now. Even the Italians wait."

Petros slumped in his chair.

Uncle Spiro patted him on the arm. "You're making good arms," he said. "Such arms could farm all day and still play the guitar all night."

Petros said, "I think I want to be a soldier."

"Being a soldier is only a job," Uncle Spiro said. "After the war, these men will go home to be builders and poets and teachers and painters. They'll play the guitar. Make families."

Petros thought of how his mama's face grew frightened

when there was talk of the soldiers. "Everyone wishes this war were over. No one wants the Italians here, but people are more scared of the Germans."

"Everyone always wishes a war were over," Uncle Spiro said. "We must learn how to avoid them before the start."

"How?"

Uncle Spiro ran his thumbs over his guitar strings. "I think about this a great deal. No answer comes."

"What exactly do you think?" Petros asked.

"I think about two men, not their countries," Uncle Spiro said. "I think if two men each think he's right and the other is wrong, does this have to lead to a fight? If one man hits the other with his fist, does this have to lead to a war? And I think, no, not if these men are smart."

Petros nodded.

"Then I think, what if one man hit the other man's son? What if the son is killed? It's too late to be smart."

The Germans of Petros's imagination didn't seem real. Only their planes were real. The bombs. But his uncle spoke only of men, and these Petros could see. "So there's war."

"Perhaps smart is not enough. We must be forgiving. Or at least, we must be willing to live with our loss. So I began to think of losses I could not forgive. The list is long."

Petros thought of losing an unfair wager. Of doing Zola's chores for three days. "So what do you think finally, Uncle?"

"I think, how can we avoid war?"

There was a certain sadness in the laughter Petros shared

with Uncle Spiro. But laughter was always good. Uncle Spiro said, "You can take some books to Zola when you go."

He led Petros into the house.

Made of soft paper, the books came from America and were written in English. Uncle Spiro spoke only Greek, and Petros spoke English but couldn't read it. The many small drawings made the stories easy to follow.

Flipping through the pages, Petros saw an undersea adventure unfolding. Petros said, "I think this story is in one of Zola's books."

"There's a puzzle for your sister," Uncle Spiro said, and handed him a cardboard box. Petros's sister, Sophie, loved these puzzles. Usually the picture they created was something she remembered and could tell Petros about.

Which meant that Petros loved them too, although he rarely sat still long enough to put them together. The picture on top of the box showed children playing in deep snow, something Petros knew about but had never seen.

Uncle Spiro took a crumpled cloth out of his pocket. He unwrapped it to reveal a glass marble. Large, a shooter. Inside, where there would ordinarily have been a thin ribbon of color, there was an American flag.

Petros gave a low whistle.

"My sister, your aunt Vivi"—Uncle always reminded him this way because Petros didn't know his aunt Vivi—"sent me books and guitar strings and a packet of tobacco. This was in the box."

Aunt Vivi stayed in America when Papa brought his family

back to Greece. Petros wished he remembered America, or even the boat trip, but he was only a baby at the time.

Uncle Spiro never left Greece, even while Papa and Aunt Vivi both lived in America. During those years, she began sending Uncle Spiro small boxes filled with interesting American things, and she hadn't stopped.

Petros knew glass marbles were easy to get in America. Still, he thought his aunt Vivi must be a woman of uncommon good taste, to have such things lying about.

Petros's pouch hung from his belt loop. He untied it and spilled his marbles at their feet. Almost unbreakable, they were made of fired clay, painted in bright colors. They looked ugly beside the glass beauty. He wrapped it up again and put it into his pouch with the others.

"You'll win every game you play now," Uncle Spiro said.

Petros shook his head. "I won't play with it."

Uncle Spiro sat back and rested his chin on his hand, frowning. "You could play with Panayoti."

"Last time I reminded him he's American too, he blacked my eye."

Uncle Spiro grunted softly. Panayoti was a hard case.

Petros scratched Lump's head one last time. "I should go home."

Uncle Spiro tied the little fellow to the table leg so only long-legged Fifi could follow Petros. Petros didn't look back at Lump's sweet dark face even once.

chapter 4

Everything Uncle Spiro said about Fifi was true. She bit, she spat, both with very little excuse. She wouldn't allow Petros to lead her with the rope. But on the walk home, he decided she must like him. Why else would she go along without coaxing? Petros strolled into the kitchen, following the smell of roasting chicken.

"What's the matter with you?" his sister scolded. She was chasing a persistent horsefly around the room with a dish towel. "Don't bring a goat in here."

Before Petros could explain he'd tried to tie her outside, Fifi bit into Sophie's skirt. "Euw! Goat slobber!" His sister ran for her room.

Petros shook his head. When Sophie turned eighteen, everyone said she'd grown up, but she acted sillier than ever.

Mama came through the doorway with a bowl full of eggs. "Take that goat outside," she said, setting the bowl on a table.

"Her name is Fifi and she bites," Petros said. He reached for her rope and she snapped at him. He drew back very quickly.

Mama clamped a hand around Fifi's mouth. Fifi sat like a

dog. One good yank on the rope and the goat allowed herself to be led outside. But when Mama tried to tie her to the rail at the doorstep, Fifi got in a good bite. "Ouch!"

Mama let go of the rope and of Fifi, both. The goat trotted over to sit down in the open doorway.

"I see what you mean," Mama said, and Petros grinned. "She could end up in my stew pot if she doesn't watch out."

Petros said, "We've traded for her. Papa wanted another female."

Mama squeezed past Fifi. "Keep her out of my kitchen— and don't take her into the garden with you."

Petros couldn't go to the garden at all, then. Fifi wanted nothing to do with the other goats, and she bit him when he tried to leave her behind with them. She bit him again while he stood trying to decide what to do about her.

"You took the wrong goat," Papa said, coming in from the garden. "Is this the trade you made?"

"Uncle Spiro was content with the trade."

Petros found it hard to meet Papa's eyes, but he threw an arm over Fifi's back and, good for them both, she didn't turn and bite him. "She'll give many babies, lots of milk."

Papa answered with a grunt.

Two things were said with this grunt. That Papa knew he'd done it deliberately. Also, this matter was not done with.

"It's suppertime," Mama said.

Petros shot her a grateful look, which she pretended not to see.

Fifi sat in the doorway all through the evening meal, looking as alert as Zola's dog, beneath the table, and far more elegant. Petros wished he'd been successful at getting Fifi into the goat pen, where she wouldn't be a constant reminder to Papa. Second best would be for Petros to find a mission to fulfill as soon as dinner was over so *he* wasn't a constant reminder. He decided to watch for the Germans.

He stationed himself in the tree just outside the front gate, on a branch overhanging the road. Petros gave a great deal of thought to the German army, slow in coming from a place not very far away.

Probably they weren't coming to Amphissa. It wasn't an important city like Athens. He had two minds about this: First, the Germans sounded interesting to him. Exciting. Second, Papa was frightened of them. Knowing that Papa was afraid of almost nothing, Petros was now frightened too.

He watched for the Germans every day, because Old Mario said the best way to avoid trouble was to see it coming. Petros had his mission to himself for nearly an hour. He ate a lot of mulberries, and dropped even more of them to Fifi, who stood below the tree.

His friend Elia came out of his house and saw Fifi beneath the tree. He walked across the road. "Are you coming down?"

"Not yet," Petros replied.

"Ouch!" The tree was easy to climb, but Fifi was quick and got in two bites before Elia was out of reach. "That goat's a mean dog."

Petros had owned this goat for less than a day, but already she was making a reputation for herself.

"Why are you here so long?" Elia asked.

"I'm watching for Germans," he told Elia in a low voice.

Elia said nothing while he rubbed his bites. Then he suggested, "We could go down to the bakery and see if there's a game."

Petros dropped a mulberry to Fifi. "Let's go."

At the back of the building, a game of marbles was in progress. Five boys, including Stavros, played in an area of hard-packed dirt.

Panayoti saw Petros coming. "Got an ugly dog there," he called.

Panayoti's fat dog barked, its neck fur standing up like a brown collar. The other boys shouted to spur it on. Fifi spread her forelegs and put her head down, ready for the fight. The dog trotted off as if it'd had something else in mind all along.

"Don't hurt Fifi's feelings," Petros said, reaching the edge of the game. "She's likely to hurt yours back."

Panayoti tried to pet her. She nipped his hand. "Yee-ouch!"

"See what I mean?"

The other boys began to tease, putting out their hands and pulling back. Petros quickly brought out his new marble.

It was an instant sensation.

All the boys wanted to roll the marble between their palms, make a test shot. Left in peace, Fifi trotted over to a weedy area for a nap. She walked in circles, trampling the grass to make her bed.

Elia peered through the marble as if he were sighting a gun. "A marvelous thing," he said, and passed the marble to Panayoti.

Panayoti looked at it critically. He didn't like things new, but if there was to be a new thing, he liked to be the one who brought it. His six-year-old brother, Hero, tugged impatiently at his sleeve.

"It's not a Greek thing," Panayoti said, and passed it to Hero.

Panayoti had been born in America and was no more or less a Greek thing than the well-traveled marble, or than Petros himself, but Petros didn't say so.

Hero looked the marble over, rolled it across his shirt as if to remove any dust that might cling, and popped it into his mouth. There was an immediate outcry. Panayoti whacked Hero on the back, and when the marble shot from Hero's mouth, he shouted, "What's the matter with you?"

Panayoti slapped Hero again on general principles. "It's a miracle you didn't swallow it."

Petros wanted to give Hero another whack. He was always swallowing something he shouldn't or putting things up his nose. He couldn't play marbles to save his life. But he was Panayoti's younger brother, and so he was tolerated.

Stavros snatched the marble up from the dirt and rubbed it in a fold of his shirt. He held it out, clean and dry, for all to see. "Let me shoot with it first, Petros," he said, his eyes sharp with greed.

chapter 5

"You can shoot with it," Petros said. Stavros could be more trouble than being first was worth. "But you can't win it from me."

Stavros, the best player by far, said, "That's how we play now. We gamble."

Petros put out his hand. "Give it back and I'll take it home."

"Don't listen to Stavros," Elia said.

Panayoti closed the argument. "If we all get to shoot with the marble, you don't have to bet."

The glass shooter improved everyone's game. They didn't stop playing until the marbles all seemed one dark color. "Where's the shooter?" Petros couldn't find it.

Elia emptied his pouch to make sure he hadn't scooped it up.

Petros saw his cousin sneaking off. "Check your pouch, Stavros."

"Why mine?" Stavros turned around, already angry. "Are you accusing me?"

All the boys stopped checking their pouches, looking on. They'd gone so still, Petros could hear their shallow breathing.

"Everyone must look," Petros said. "But you're in the greatest hurry to go home." He made fists. "We should check yours first."

Stavros shoved Petros, and Petros pushed back.

At first that's all they did, push and yell insults. Petros had the better insults, or maybe a better memory, and hit a sensitive nerve. Stavros launched himself at Petros, knocking him to the ground. The boys rolled in the dirt, getting in punches when they could.

The other boys shouted advice to both. Panayoti's dog yapped. Fifi's voice rose in an alarmed *meh-eh-eh, meh-eh-eh,* and once she reached into the fray to nip. She got Petros.

The string on Stavros's pouch broke, spilling the marbles between them. They felt like pebbles under Petros's ribs and shoulders, but he hardly knew it. He gave back as many blows as he'd gotten. Hitting fast and furiously, he bloodied Stavros's nose. Stavros returned the favor.

Petros hardly noticed when the shouts died away and the dog barked more ravenously than before.

A stranger snatched him up by the neck and grabbed Stavros as well, separating them roughly. "Stop it," he told them. "We're at war already! Don't fight among yourselves."

Petros stopped fighting right away, not because the stranger scolded but because he stank. His matted hair and beard clung to his head like a scarf of sheep's wool. His face and body were dirty and sunburned, his nose and shoulders blistered and scabbed over. He wore only the ragged remains of his trousers.

His feet were wrapped in rags. Bloody rags.

After one long look at him, Petros and Stravros both struggled to escape. "Quit!" the stranger shouted, so hard his voice failed and the rest of what he said came out in a whisper. "Stavros, Petros, stop it."

Petros was frightened into struggling even harder. The stranger stood firm, holding Petros in place with only a grip on his shirt collar.

Stavros froze, still gripped about the neck. "Lambros? Is that you?"

"Of course it's me." The stranger let go of them. "Don't you recognize your own brother?"

Petros stared. Could this filthy, wrecked creature be the same Lambros whose daring assaults on the Italian army were so dramatic that word of his courage reached the village? Whose adventures were told and retold on the verandas? Only nineteen and already he was a hero.

"Lambros." Petros was sickened to see the cuts on his hands, the torn nails. How could this happen to him?

Stavros said, "Your feet, Lambros. Where are your boots?"

"Gone." Lambros didn't wait but limped forward a few steps. "It's enough to know for now. Let's go home."

Stavros moved to put his arm about Lambros's waist, to be his crutch. Lambros stopped him, saying, "Don't come so close. I'm covered with lice. Walk with me, but keep your distance."

The boys followed Lambros.

Petros snatched up the spilled marbles. His glass marble

was now among them. As for the rest, there remained just enough evening light to tell them apart.

He stuffed his own marbles into his pouch, glad for the moment to himself. The vision that was Lambros had shaken him. He dropped Stavros's marbles into his pocket and hurried to catch up.

Elia pointed to Lambros's swollen hands and asked, "What happened to you?"

"Little enough," Lambros said as Petros joined them, "considering all that might have happened."

"Where's the rest of your company?" Panayoti asked.

"On their way home, the lucky ones. Has no one else returned from the north?"

"No one yet," Panayoti replied.

"Then you must all go home now and give warning," Lambros said, his voice rising like an alarm. "Tell your families the Germans are near."

"They've been coming for nearly a month," Petros said. "Even the Italians aren't expecting them."

"Go tell your father now," Lambros yelled, in a voice sharp with the pain of his feet and hands.

Petros ran, but not because news of the Germans was frightening or even important. His legs had wanted to carry him away since he'd laid eyes on Lambros. Only the fact that the other boys had not run made him stay.

Petros ran, his own heartbeat loud in his ears. With Elia, he raced through the gathering darkness, Fifi close behind them.

chapter 6

Petros and Elia ran recklessly, tripping over rocks, with only the pale moonlight to guide them. By the time they pelted alongside the rock wall of Petros's home, both had scraped knees and palms.

When Elia veered off, Petros headed straight for his own gate, a little farther along the road. Panting, he hurried first to the veranda. His father could ordinarily be found there at this hour, smoking a cigarette and playing cards. Perhaps doing card tricks.

Tonight, no one sat outside. Not Papa. Not Zola. Not Old Mario.

Poking his face into the front room, Petros blinked against the lamplight. His sister and Elia's sister, Maria, sat at the card table, putting the puzzle together. "Sophie, where's Papa?"

Neither of them looked up. "Down the well."

"Why?"

"One of the tributaries has gone dry," Sophie said briskly. "Get that goat out of here."

Petros heard Mama talking to her friends as they worked

on their knitting in the kitchen. To take his sister's mind off Fifi as he cut through, he said, "Lambros has come home."

Sophie gave him a sharp glance. "Has he been injured?"

"His feet are bleeding," he said.

"Mama," Sophie cried. She leaped off the divan and followed him to the kitchen, wailing, "Mama, Lambros is dying!"

Clattering over the marble floor, Fifi stayed right behind Petros as he dashed past Mama and Elia's mother and grandmother—all of them suddenly talking at once. Petros let the kitchen door slam against the house as he burst through.

Petros slowed, letting his eyes get used to the darkness again. He saw the white of Zola's dog turn at the sound of Fifi's hooves on the gravel. He didn't bark. He didn't care to fight a goat.

Old Mario and Zola stood looking down the well. Zola was very much the taller of the two. Petros crossed to Old Mario's side, and they stood shoulder to shoulder. Only recently he'd noticed he was for the first time as tall as someone who wasn't a child. He still liked the novelty of it.

A great deal of cold air rose from the well. This was welcome in the heat of daylight, but now it chilled Petros as he leaped up to cling to the thick rock wall, letting his feet hang and his weight rest on his forearms.

The mouth of the well was as big across as Mama's kitchen, to accommodate the copper buckets, barrel-shaped, but larger. Petros looked down, but there was only the cold and greater darkness. He asked, "Papa climbed down?"

Zola said, "He wants to see if a tunnel has collapsed." This was delivered in the tone of superior logic that Zola had adopted at the old age of fifteen.

Petros could rarely hear this tone without arguing with it. "There's still plenty of water." There were several tunnels bringing water to the well.

He'd been down below to stand hunched over in one of these only once, carrying a tool to Papa when he was making a repair. It wouldn't trouble him if he never had to go below again. It had been dark, except for Papa's lamp, and cold. Too cold.

"You made a lucky escape," Zola said.

When Petros looked the question at him, Zola said, "Papa's thinking about bigger things than trading goats."

At a shout from deep within, Zola hurried to the pump house and threw the switch. The motor started with a *putt-putt-putt,* and the belt whined as it turned. The tarnished green buckets jerked, then began to move, the chain creaking as it stretched over the axle.

When the buckets reached the top, water spilled into the reservoir and trickled along tiled gutters to the garden. The empty buckets shifted lower, then lower still, working up to a steady pace. Curious, Fifi put her front hooves up against the well.

"How do we fix a tunnel?" Petros asked Old Mario. The old man made a rolling motion with one hand that suggested a great deal of trouble.

Papa emerged from the darkness, ghostly. He stood on the

edge of one of the buckets, holding on to the chain, coming up and up, until he could step onto the rock wall circling the well. His wet shirt hung nearly to his knees. He jumped to the ground, shivering like a wet dog.

Petros began, "Papa—"

"Bring me a dry shirt. Two dry shirts." Papa shook himself, spraying icy water over everyone. "Go."

Petros ran through the kitchen with Fifi at his heels. When the women called to him, he shouted, "Elia saw him too," over his shoulder. In the bedroom, he rummaged through his father's drawers for shirts.

Fifi looked as if she knew what Petros needed to do. He liked this about her. She was at least as good as the dog. Better, because the dog only followed Zola, when he followed at all.

Mama and Grandmother Lemos reached for Petros as he ran past again. Elia's mother spoke into the phone. Petros ducked out the back door.

Papa wore the dry pants he'd taken off before going into the well. He shivered so hard he steadied himself with a hand on Zola's shoulder to pull on his socks.

"This goat follows you like a dog," he said as the first dry shirt went over his head. "Are you sure she's a goat?"

"She bites like a goat," Petros said, reminded that he was about to be in big trouble. "But then, so does Zola's dog."

Papa pulled on the second shirt, now walking toward the house. "If she eats like Zola's dog," he said, "she'd better scare cats away from the chicken house."

Following Papa, Petros said, "She's already scared off a dog," and made Papa laugh. He saw Elia's mother and grandmother crossing the road, surely to get Elia's side of the story. "Papa, I saw Lam—"

From the back steps, Sophie cried out, "Papa, Lambros is dying."

Petros shouted, "I was to tell!"

Papa turned to Petros. "Where did you see Lambros?"

Old Mario snuffed out the lamp and hurried to join them. Petros said, "He came out of the woods near the bakery. I'm to tell you the Germans are coming. They're close."

Papa rushed into the house, impatiently yanking Petros along. Zola followed, peppering Petros with questions. "What else did he say? Where are the Germans exactly? Were any of the other men from the village with him—the soldiers?"

chapter 7

Petros offered less-careful information as the family gathered around him. "Lambros looks like a wild man," he said. "Half naked. His feet are torn—"

"You said he was dying," Sophie accused him.

"*You* said he was dying," Petros said. "*I* said his feet were bleeding."

"What if it's true?" Mama asked. "About the Germans."

"I need to know more," Papa said. "I'll go speak to him."

"We'll go together," Old Mario said.

"Let me go too." This was Petros and Zola together.

"Don't be gone long," Mama said, looking worried.

"Let me go," Zola said.

Petros wanted to plead but stood quiet. The goat began to chew on his shirttail, and he slapped at her. He was nipped in return.

Old Mario said, "Boys must see what it means to be at war."

"He's my cousin too," Sophie protested.

"No one needs to see war," Mama argued.

But Papa told them, "While we're gone, bring everything of our life in America to the kitchen. Letters. Books. Clothing. Everything."

"Not dresses," Sophie said, because she'd gotten a dress through the mail from New York City only the week before.

"From this moment, we don't care about books or languages," Papa said. "We have no interest in travel or politics."

Zola couldn't believe it. "What kind of Greek is that?"

"The rare kind we'll pretend to be," Papa said. "The Germans can't find anything to set us apart from the other villagers. Nothing to give us away."

This felt wrong to Petros. It was as if Papa had agreed with the boys in the village all along. His children were never really Greek.

Zola said, "Surely other families have some things from America."

"Those things make men ask too many questions," Papa said. "I don't want the Germans to take an interest in me or my Greek family."

"If they come," Zola said, as if Lambros could be wrong.

"If they come," Papa said in a way meant to give Zola something to think about, "they'll search this house."

Petros understood. Not all the villagers owned large farms or fine houses.

"My dress," Sophie said, looking to Mama.

"We'll bury it," Papa said.

On a gasp from Sophie, Mama said, "We'll keep it for later."

"On second thought, the boys will come," Papa said. "Sophie, help your mother."

Sophie stamped her foot.

At the door, Papa stopped and said, "No one here speaks English. Not German. Not Albanian or French. Whether or not the Germans are here, we speak Greek and only Greek."

"What about Italian, Papa?" This was Zola.

"Greek. It's enough."

Petros couldn't speak all these languages, mainly because he'd never cared to learn. Because everyone else in the house spoke English, he'd learned a little. Enough to enjoy stories. He saw no reason to bother about a third and fourth and fifth language when he spoke to the same people every day.

Things had changed. Where once Zola thought him too lazy to learn and perhaps a little stupid because he didn't want to, Petros now possessed a talent—the one way he couldn't help but stay out of trouble.

Papa chased the goat away as they left the yard.

He never used to shut the gates at night. Now he wrapped the chain around the bars in a figure eight before he sat down to dinner. Things had changed.

Only weeks ago, Elia and his grandfather would come over to sit on the porch in the evening. The men would play cards. Sometimes Elia's father came too. But then he'd said admiring things about the Germans, and Papa sat very quiet. Old Mario and even Elia's grandfather ignored his remarks.

One night Papa did one of his card tricks, betting a drachma that no one could tell how he did it. It was harmless, the drachma nearly worthless. But Elia's father lost his drachma and got angry over it. Papa gave it back, which made him angrier still. Elia's father began to stay home, and so did Grandfather Lemos. Everything had changed.

Skinny Fifi stepped through the gate and followed at a distance.

On the walk to his sister's house in the village, Papa set a fast pace. Zola grumbled a little about the new rules. "What's the good of learning languages if I can't use them?"

"You don't have to look smart to be smart," Papa said over his shoulder.

"I may have to hide that I'm American," Zola argued, "but doesn't that mean I could be proud I'm Greek?"

"Be proud," Old Mario said, "but also be quiet about it."

"We could hang a Greek flag from the chimney," Zola said. "That's something Americans wouldn't be expected to do."

"Don't waste my breath." Old Mario hurried to keep up with Papa.

"We're a family thinking about farming. And surviving," Papa said. "We don't hang flags. We hope this war will pass like a storm."

Zola opened his mouth to argue this but shut it again. Petros knew the sign of an idea occurring to his brother. This had not changed.

"Why did we leave America?" Petros asked, thinking most

of what they had to hide was there to begin with. And so were they. To begin with.

"Business was bad for too long," Papa said. He'd lost his grocery store in a time when no one paid what they owed him, and he still felt this wound deeply. "We were better off here until this war. Now we've missed our chance to go back."

Petros remembered a time at the dinner table—he remembered the lemon flavor of the roast chicken going sour in his mouth—Papa wanted to return to America by boat. They'd made enough money on the farm to start over, and he was ready to go.

Zola and Sophie cheered. Sometimes Petros thought they pretended to remember America better than they really did, but he also liked the little he knew about—soft paper books and glass marbles and toy trucks.

Before he could decide *he* wanted to go, Mama said she'd heard too many stories on the radio of German U-boats sinking ships. Zola argued they heard only of the ones that sank, not of the ones to reach a port, but Mama still worried.

Petros didn't want to end up as fish food, and secretly he'd sided with Mama. After many such evenings of talk that ended in shouting and tears, they dropped the subject. In the back of his mind now, he could see their boat safely passing the Statue of Liberty—it was the subject of one of Sophie's puzzles—and his family wasn't on it. He was sorry he hadn't secretly sided with Papa.

"Why is it so bad to be American?" Petros asked.

"Not bad," Old Mario said. "Dangerous."

"Dangerous, then," Petros said. "Americans aren't fighting."

Papa said, "The Greeks said they weren't fighting either."

Zola said, "Already the Americans defend the coastlines in Greenland and Nova Scotia against the Axis. That's why Greece had to fight. To keep the Germans out." The family had all heard this report from Cairo the week before, but Petros didn't feel like teasing his brother.

The village shops were dark, but lights showed in every window of the house where his cousins lived. They found Stavros sitting in the shadows outside.

chapter 8

Papa said, "Is your brother home?"

Stavros nodded. "The men are washing him down with kerosene to kill the lice."

Stavros's grandmother on his father's side, called Auntie by most people, opened the door to Papa's knock. Half the village seemed to be gathered in the kitchen, everyone talking at once.

Old Mario followed Papa. Zola and his dog were right behind Old Mario. Papa turned Zola around and pushed him back outside. "When I call you."

Zola and Petros looked in through the window.

When someone opened the door to toss out the end of a cigarette—the red cinder of it arced like a shooting star—Zola slipped inside.

The dog sat down at the door. Petros wanted to sneak in too. If the dog remained outside so quietly, perhaps Fifi would do the same. He decided to wait a minute or two and see how things worked out for his brother. It took only one worm to bait a hook.

Zola didn't get thrown out and didn't get thrown out, and still Petros didn't make a move to go inside. He was torn between wanting to stand beside Papa and the worrying sight of Stavros sitting alone.

He would've let Stavros sulk, but today they'd seen Lambros's feet. Baby chickens sometimes got a disease where they pecked each other until they bled, often until they died. Lambros's feet had looked that bad.

Stavros moved to the rock wall bordering another property.

He didn't look welcoming. Petros strolled over there anyway, with Fifi nibbling at his sleeve. Stavros remained with his back turned, so Petros spoke to the back of him. "Why are you over here?"

"He's crazy, I think," Stavros said. He wiped his face with his arm.

"He looked it," Petros agreed. Then he realized Stavros hoped he'd say otherwise.

"He says he climbed the Needle," Stavros said. "To get away from the Germans, he climbed to the top."

The Needle was a narrow spike of marbled rock, all that remained of a mountain after the miners were finished with it. This tall spike was made up of smooth cold sides and sharp edges, like the needle Papa used to mend their leather sandals.

Before the war, men *tried* to climb the Needle. Many of them fell to their death. But some climbers lived to tell of searching for a crevice in the marble, of gripping it with sweaty hands.

Or men told of resting in the branches of scrubby twisted little trees sprouting like horns from those crevices. Petros didn't know if he could rest, dangling hundreds of feet from the ground in such a way.

He thought Lambros might not have meant he'd climbed alone. Those who were successful had climbed as a team. But to tackle the Needle at all, there must be ropes.

To tie ropes, the climber pounded in hooks.

To pound hooks, a man needed a hammer. Petros said, "Did he have a hammer?"

"Do you think he could make that much noise?" Stavros said, still looking out into the night. "The soldiers would have shot him dead."

So. No hammer. "Perhaps there are some old hooks still there."

"He used the cracks in the rock," Stavros said, a bullying tone creeping into his voice. To say Lambros climbed the Needle, with hooks or without, was to say he scaled the face of a wall, clinging like a spider.

"He knew who we were, all of us," Petros said. "He isn't crazy. And he's not a liar."

Stavros wiped his face again. "He talks to the dead. He's crazy."

"That's not crazy," Petros said stoutly, thinking of Mama's mother. "My grandmother Popi speaks to the dead." He didn't say she only did so in church.

Pretending not to see his cousin's tears, Petros pulled

Stavros's marbles out of his pockets. He set them in the shallow bowl of a rock.

"When he goes into the mountains, I'm going with him," Stavros said. Petros dug the toe of his sandal into the dirt, thinking this might be true. Then again, it might not.

"Who'll take care of your family?" There were his mother, Aunt Hypatia, who was Papa's sister, and his grandmother, Auntie.

Stavros didn't answer this. He poked Petros. "Are you leaving tonight with the others?"

"Leaving?" Fifi sat down as if she'd heard something interesting.

"Panayoti and his family are going. He wouldn't say where, but Mama said it would be Cephalonia. They have family there."

"Only Panayoti is American," Petros said.

Stavros shot him a look. "His family won't send him away alone."

"Who'll run the bakery?" he asked, because it was Panayoti's family's business.

"Who cares?" Stavros said.

"We're not leaving," Petros said.

"But you're Americans. The Germans shoot Americans."

Petros felt the hair stand on his arms, but he hoped Stavros was just saying this because he was still a little angry. Stavros could stay mad longer than anyone Petros knew.

"Did you find your marble?" Stavros asked him.

"You got in two very good hits," Petros said, to let Stavros know there were no hard feelings.

"Hah," Stavros said. Ants could crawl over him, bite him even, and he wouldn't give in—Petros knew this about him.

chapter 9

As they started the walk home, Zola whispered, "Lambros said the German soldiers look like they're made of iron."

A pleasant shiver ran up Petros's back.

Zola said, "The Germans climb the hills at the border with tanks. Too many soldiers to count are spilling out of big trucks that followed the tanks."

"What then?"

"They have guns that spit bullets so fast that a line of men can be mowed down in a breath." Petros let these pictures play in his imagination, scary but exciting too.

Zola's whispers became more worrying. He said Lambros had walked all the way from Marathon because he'd dreamed of a death in the family. He cried like a baby to find all of them well.

Petros squirmed. If Lambros cried, what would anyone else do?

"We fought well," Petros said. "I heard it on the radio. Why didn't we win?"

Papa said, "Our army is small. Our planes are too old to stop the Germans."

Petros said, "So Lambros and the others hide in the mountains?"

"The Germans shoot or make slaves of other countries' soldiers—they'll do the same to ours," Zola said angrily. "Lambros can't stay here."

"From now on our army fights dressed like shepherds," Papa said. "Bravery isn't enough. They must have cards up their sleeves."

Petros remembered the hungry Italian soldiers who stole eggs and green tomatoes. "How will they eat?"

"There's the problem," Papa said. "They won't find it easy to live off the land, especially if they're moving or hiding."

Old Mario said, "We won't find it easy to live off the land either, if the Germans are taking the farmer's machetes and pitchforks."

This was something else they'd learned from the radio. Anything likely to be used as a weapon was being taken away. Old Mario urged Papa to take Lambros's advice, to do as Panayoti's family was doing, strike out for one of the islands until the war was over.

"And when we get there, then what?" Papa said. "We must stay where we are and be careful not to draw attention to ourselves."

Lambros was afraid the Germans would send Americans north to the concentration camps. Petros thought this sounded unlikely. But then, nearly everything he heard about the Germans sounded unlikely. Only the fact that he heard it straight off the radio made any of it believable at all.

Papa said they had to stay where they were. Mama's family lived in Athens, where matters were worse—people were hungry and lived in great fear. There were small cells of Greek political parties that hoped to become important to the Germans and so couldn't be trusted. Possibly Mama's mother and brothers were right now planning their journey to Amphissa.

As this back-and-forth went on with Old Mario, Petros learned Papa had argued with his sister. She'd brought her sons to live here with Auntie, her husband's mother, some years ago. In this way, Papa could look after them all. But Aunt Hypatia had made up her mind to follow Lambros to the mountains to nurse the injured men. Papa didn't like it.

"What about Stavros?" Petros asked. "Will he go with Aunt Hypatia?"

"He'll stay here with Auntie," Zola said, full of knowing. "She's too old to be alone. They'll look after each other."

At home, letters and photos and maps were piled on the kitchen table. Sophie's fancy dolls, Mama's alligator purse, and several pairs of shoes, including Papa's and Zola's best, appeared to be waiting for a bus.

Petros picked up his tractor. Papa read what remained of the lettering on the side, "John Deere," and added, "Put it on the table."

Petros did, very reluctantly. He'd outgrown playing with it anyway, he reminded himself. "Panayoti and his family have gone," he said to Mama.

"He's right," Papa said. He emptied the coal scuttle into the stove, building up the fire. "They're going into hiding."

"Cephalonia?" his mother whispered, making Petros hope they'd go there. To an island west of the mainland, where pirates used to hide in the caves off the sea.

"I can't feed my family in a cave," Papa said.

He tossed a handful of letters into the stove, making Mama gasp. Sophie, her eyes red-rimmed from crying, came into the kitchen at the same moment. She shrieked.

"You don't remember what these people look like," Papa said.

"I do too." Sophie looked nearly as fierce as Papa. "When I read the letters, I can see them." Mama was as upset as Sophie, but she pushed her out of the room and down the hall.

Papa said, "Zola, Petros, help your mother and sister. Find everything in your room that has the faintest trace of English lettering."

Papa stacked the newspapers he and Zola read from, anti-German. A Greek flag was printed on the front, a bright spot of blue and white on an otherwise gray paper. Mama wrapped the Sunday dinner plates in them and placed the dishes in baskets with lids.

Most of their books were to be buried, because they

wouldn't burn easily. But Papa burned Uncle Spiro's soft paper books. Zola argued, "I should take them back to Uncle Spiro."

"We burn them or he does," Papa said. "It makes no difference."

Petros riffled the pages of one he hadn't read yet. Perhaps some things could be burned tomorrow. When Papa left the kitchen, he told Mama, "I'd like to look at this."

Mama said, "I feel the same way about my *Life* magazines, but I burn them all the more quickly." Petros sighed. So much for that.

Zola silently burned his U.S. state maps and a box of colored pencils. Petros hated to see the pencils go, but he sacrificed a pink rubber ball with a lot of bounce left in it—a word printed on it in English doomed it.

In the next hour, Sophie got in trouble for complaining and Zola made Papa angry when he spoke English. Zola handed over a metal bank shaped like a man, wearing boots, a big hat, guns on his hips, and a star on his vest. Petros didn't ask what this figure was called—it wasn't a Greek word. He gave up his small cars, toys from America, and a red fire engine, something he'd never seen in real life. Metal toys would be buried.

Then Sophie handed him his fuzzy bear. He pretended not to mind, but he'd slept with it for as long as he could remember, rubbing his thumb over one of its glass eyes in the darkness. "Do we bury this?" he asked Mama, hoping she wouldn't toss it right into the stove.

"A baby's toy," Zola said, making Petros feel ashamed.

"I remember *you* were a baby once," Mama said.

"Papa said we bury things of value," Zola said.

"I love this bear," Mama said with a wink at Petros. "Don't put it in a basket—I don't want bugs to eat it. Put it in the metal box with your sister's dresses and the passports."

"I'm not saving the life of a toy," Zola said, handing over some model ships he'd made himself by gluing the many wooden pieces together and then painting them. They weren't for play but for looking at.

"One more sneer and you'll be sorry," Mama said.

But Zola had already made Petros feel he should be more of a man. Even Mama, well-meaning as she was, made him feel childish.

When Zola found a big paper flag and hid it, Petros said nothing. It wasn't American anyway. It was a Greek flag left over from the part Petros had played in a school assembly, rolled up and forgotten once it had fallen behind some of the books on the shelf. While it truly never *belonged* to anyone, Zola claimed it, spreading the stiff paper flat under his mattress with a sweep of his arm.

Petros said nothing.

chapter 10

It was past midnight when Old Mario looked through the kitchen door to remind them of the time. Until then, Petros had been distracted from how tired he felt. Now he only wanted to fall into bed.

"You two start holes below the windows," Papa said to Petros and Zola. "Try not to disturb the bushes, but dig deep."

"Papa, it's dark outside," Petros said.

"How much light do you need to dig a hole?"

Petros hadn't known Old Mario had been digging all this time, working by moonlight. He was amazed to see a fresh ditch running from the kitchen door to the front corner of the house. He went for more shovels.

Papa sent him back to the shed. "Find buckets to put the dirt into. Bring the other wheelbarrow."

Everyone either dug or moved dirt or buried something. Zola's dog got the idea and worked like a machine, furiously pelting soft garden dirt out between his back legs. He didn't dig deep, but he started holes very well, and Petros soon began to follow him.

Petros realized he'd always been asleep at this hour. "What time is it?" he asked Zola, who stood knee-deep in a hole.

"Late. Or perhaps it's early."

"Put some shoulder into it," Old Mario scolded as he walked past them. "It won't be dark all day."

Petros dug harder.

After a time, he asked, "Do you think Uncle Spiro knows the Germans are so near?"

"Don't worry—he always knows things," Zola said.

When there was no place left to dig alongside the house, Papa dug behind the feed shed. He buried his guns, both of them, and three machetes covered in oilcloth. The entire night passed before Papa felt satisfied their house looked like any other.

But there was more work to be done. As the sun came up, Papa spread compost to disguise the freshly dug graves of their belongings. A few of the plants looked wilted, the roots disturbed by the digging. Old Mario carried water to revive them.

Wheelbarrow loads of dirt were left over, dirt that would never fit back into the holes. Mama and Sophie shoveled this dirt between the garden rows. Mama's feet dragged when she walked, and she stopped sometimes to lean against her shovel.

"How many more?" Sophie asked. The palms of her hands were red with soreness. She wasn't accustomed to digging.

"Stop now," Mama said. "They could ask how you made blisters."

They. The German soldiers towered in Petros's imagination, broad but flat. Now, more than during the night, as they worked they listened for the sound of the Germans' arrival, worried they'd come too soon.

"Go inside and start breakfast," Mama told Sophie.

"I'm too tired to eat," Sophie moaned.

"It'll help," Mama said. "We have more to do."

Petros and Zola mixed the fresh dirt with the compost. Petros discovered the weights his own arms and legs had become. He'd never stayed up all night before.

When they went inside to eat, there was no polenta, no raisins. Sophie gave them milk and coffee in which to dip dry bread. Mama sliced hard cheese to make the bread more interesting.

Papa told them he'd put the radio in the cellar room.

"Why?" Petros asked.

"Because radios will be taken away," Papa said. "The Germans won't want us to have any news of the war."

"How *will* we get news?" Zola wanted to know.

"The news is coming to us," Papa said.

"Yanni and Seraphina are old friends," Mama said, speaking of Elia's grandparents across the road. "They already know we have a radio."

No one said it, but they all knew Papa had disagreed with Elia's father. The rest of the Lemos family was practically as dear to them as Stavros and his family. Petros had known them just as long and eaten at their table at least as often.

When Petros put his arms on the table to rest his head, Mama didn't scold, but Sophie poked him with a sharp finger. "Sit up," she said. "You remind me how much I want to sleep."

"We have to go on as if this were any other day," Papa said. "No English. Forget it all." During the night, Zola, Sophie, and Petros had all earned slaps. Petros didn't think he would have any more trouble speaking only Greek.

Everyone rose slowly, as if trying to remember what they did any other day. Petros fed the pig and chickens. Zola tossed hay into the goats' pen. Old Mario laid the hoes over his shoulder, making things ready for the others to join him in the garden.

Fresh dark soil lay where it had been spilled. There was something unreal about this idea of war. Even though Petros had sore muscles from too many hours of digging, the memory of it already felt like a dream. But the soil, that was real. No one talked.

So tired they were nearly sick, they raked through the dirt, walking over it so the garden merely looked well-tended.

chapter 11

Petros's garden lay in the poorest corner of the farm, a little way from the arbor. He'd badgered Papa for it. Zola had given him a dozen tomato plants and six bell pepper plants grown for Papa.

Petros also seeded several rows of onions and garlic, but only a few straggly shoots had come up. The rocky patch didn't even encourage weeds. It needed a great deal of improvement to produce anything. He was glad to see dark hills of fresh soil at the ends of his rows.

He raked the dirt in, then carried water and dribbled it slowly around the seedlings. Pouring too fast might knock them down, and if the water ran off to soak the dirt where nothing grew, carrying the pail was wasted effort. But also he moved slowly. He sat down to work when he could, where only a day ago he would have bent at the waist.

An hour later, Old Mario started the well, and more water began to trickle into Petros's garden, making the soil muddy. Although Papa hardly ever turned on the well before the sun was going down, when the water came, it meant the day's work was finished.

The singsong whine of the belt that worked the well could be heard in the background, like the static on a radio. The birds sang. Tin cans, strung between the plants to keep the birds and mice away, clanked as the men brushed against them.

All of these together were the sound of peace.

Returning to the yard, Petros found that Fifi had escaped the goat pen, climbing the fence like a ladder and falling over the top. Papa couldn't catch her.

Old Mario came to help, and with all three of them chasing her like a pack of weary dogs, Petros shut her in again. Fifi bit him as he reached through the fencing for the rope around her neck and tethered her.

"I think," Papa said, "your uncle got the best of the bargain." Petros grinned and scratched Fifi behind the ears. She nipped him again.

As Zola shut the door on the seedling shed, Papa said, "We're ready."

Zola said, "If only we knew how far away the Germans are." All their eyes strayed to the house, where the radio was hidden beneath Zola and Petros's room.

Aunt Hypatia came down the road then, carrying a rolled blanket on her back and string sacks filled to bulging. Papa gave her the large male kid, which would feed the men when they got to the mountains. Petros was glad he'd already taken Lump to Uncle Spiro.

Lambros, packed like a mule, followed at a distance. He'd

keep an eye on his mother, but they couldn't walk together until she left the road, well past Uncle Spiro's farm.

After all the good-byes, Petros's own mama still worked in her kitchen. She'd kiss him on the forehead when she sent him to bed that night. Petros knew this wasn't true for Stavros anymore. For an instant he fought an unnamed fear—and won, pushing it back into a dark corner of his heart.

When Aunt Hypatia and Lambros were out of sight, Papa sent Petros to turn off the well.

Ordinarily Petros played with Elia during the afternoon rest period, but today Elia didn't show up. Just as well, Petros thought as he sat down to a late meal he was too tired to eat. Today he might do as Papa usually did, and nap.

"I'm going to have a look around," Papa said, scraping his plate of bread and tomato salad clean.

"I'll go with you," Old Mario said, following him to the door. "Four ears hear better than two."

"Rest," Papa said to him. "If the Germans pass this way, you must be the man they talk to."

"Papa," Zola protested. Petros knew this look. His brother wanted to be appointed the man of the house.

"Zola, go shift everything around in your room. If you can see an outline of your books, wipe the shelves."

Zola nodded, standing taller. "I'll make it seem like nothing has changed."

Mama pulled at Papa's sleeve. "Perhaps you shouldn't go to the village today."

"Just today," Papa said, "or tomorrow too? Or next week?"

"We don't know when they'll come," Mama said.

"Exactly. I know this is hard," Papa said. "We're frightened, but not more frightened than the Lemos family across the street. We're ordinary Greeks, who are sorry this war has moved into our parlor."

"Ordinary Greeks," Mama muttered as Papa and Old Mario crossed the yard, deep in conversation. "The man has no idea how funny he is."

As Papa got into his truck and drove away, Fifi started to climb over the fence again. Old Mario stopped by the goat pen and she dropped to the ground, following him on her side of the fence. Petros perked up. Old Mario knew magic words.

"What are you doing, Petros?" Sophie asked, in that way that meant she had an unpleasant job in mind for him.

"I'm helping Zola."

"I don't need your help," Zola said.

Petros sighed. The problem of being the younger brother was the older brother.

A couple of hours later, when Papa returned, he told them Panayoti's family had gone during the night. Many other families had gone, but the village would miss businesspeople most. The ice factory before, now the shoemaker, the dry goods store, the ironworker.

"Who will bake?" Mama wanted to know.

"The Basilises' girls will go into business for themselves," Papa said.

"How will people pay?"

"Anything you buy," Papa said, "you must expect to offer an equal weight in paper money. Twenty ounces of bread, twenty ounces of drachmas." Except for Mama, who drew in a breath, everyone around the table fell quiet.

"Where is Zola?" Papa asked.

"Sleeping," Mama said, almost hungrily.

"The Germans?" Old Mario asked finally.

"No one knows," Papa said.

"It doesn't matter," Mama said. "We have to rest."

Everyone headed for their beds. Today even Petros wanted to sleep.

Zola was curled in the middle of his bed, snoring.

The entire floor shone from polishing. Zola had moved his bed over the trapdoor to the cellar, and the rug to the other end of the room. If the Germans came, they'd see the rug, flip it up, and find nothing.

Petros fell onto his bed, asleep before his head hit the pillow.

chapter 12

When the family got up that evening, still as quiet as sleep-walkers, Elia was already waiting for Petros on the veranda. "We could watch the road."

Petros woke up. "We'll see the Germans coming." They pelted toward the mulberry tree, Fifi trotting along behind them.

Stavros walked out from the village to join them. "There's no one at the bakery except those two Medusas making bread."

They climbed, daring each other to go higher. The danger of this inspired them to screaming and laughter and ever greater feats of bravery. They stuffed themselves on the berries, purple juice staining their lips and fingers.

As it grew dark, Old Mario walked to the pump house and flipped the switch on. The diesel motor started with a *putt-putt-putt* before settling into an effortless hum. Likewise, the belt screamed, then shifted into a fading whine as it started to crank. The buckets sprang into motion, clanking softly as they were carried down to fill with water and rise again. In a few minutes, water would course through tile gutters to water the farthest corners of the garden.

The boys settled on sturdier branches and made a game of trying to throw mulberries into Fifi's open mouth, like dropping pebbles into a jar.

The American teacher came bicycling along the road.

The boys hid among the leaves, shushing each other but also making enough noise to be noticed. The goat stood with forefeet propped high on the tree trunk, begging for more mulberries, but even this sight failed to interest the teacher.

It was a little disappointing.

Zola came out to ask them to fill a can with berries for him. His dog looked up, but not like Fifi, as if they had anything of value up there.

"What do you want them for?" Petros asked as Elia dropped berries. Fifi ate them as fast as Zola could reach for them, and he got nipped twice to gain a handful of berries.

He went back to the house, complaining about the goat.

"He's up to something," Petros said when he realized Zola had not answered him. Stavros shrugged in a way that clearly meant he cared about nothing Zola would be up to.

Elia said, "We're up to something too." He tucked himself into the branches with the thickest clumps of leaves, where he couldn't be seen.

The Russian family slowly approached. They'd loaded a wheelbarrow with their belongings, or at least as much as they could carry. Blanket rolls were tied around their waists.

"Are you boys playing a game?" the husband asked them as they reached the tree.

"We're watching the road," Petros said.

"See anything worth telling?"

Elia came out of his hiding place. "Not yet."

The wife asked if Petros and his family were leaving. "They're Greek," Stavros said. To this the couple said nothing. They kept going.

But a little ways off, the husband shook his head. Petros couldn't remember living anywhere but Greece. Being American felt as real to him as the looming German army. In fact, the war felt more real. He had blisters now.

Shortly after that, an English family, the Walkers, came down the road. The parents were on foot but the children rode bicycles. One of the girls had been a classmate a month ago. She waved when she saw the boys jump down to meet them.

Each bicycle carried bundles in the basket in front and a bedroll on the back fender. The parents were also bundled. This family had lived in Amphissa as long as Petros. Their Greek was excellent.

"Why is everyone going now? Why not sooner?" Stavros asked.

"We thought Amphissa would remain safe," Mr. Walker said without stopping. He had something to do with old relics, always digging, then sitting outside brushing away the dirt. His face was browned, his hair as light as any German's.

Mrs. Walker said, "What's here? No boats, no bridges. Who thought of the mountains?"

Papa, Petros thought. Papa knew right away their army

would hide in the mountains. It gave him a little thrill, remembering. But also a nagging feeling.

Mr. Walker said, "Petros, is your family staying?"

The concern on the Englishman's face bothered Petros. Elia too, because he said, "They've hidden everything not Greek."

"Good luck to you," Mr. Walker said, hurrying his family along.

Fifi followed them a little way, nibbling on the corner of Mr. Walker's pack. "Where can they go?" Elia said.

"With enough money, away," Stavros said.

Petros said, "They can't go north where the Germans are. Zola says in Crete people book passage to Egypt. From there, they hope to get home."

"Crete will sink with the weight of so many people," Stavros said, his eyebrows drawn together. "I'm going home."

Petros thought his cousin had begun to worry about his mother and brother. He wouldn't even know when they'd reached safety.

The parade slowed to a trickle of passersby as night fell and Fifi curled up at the gate to sleep. Twice more Petros was asked when he would go. Elia spoke on his behalf, saying, "He's Greek."

The more Elia made this claim, the less Greek Petros felt.

When Elia was called home later in the evening, Petros wondered what fate had befallen Zola. He found his brother in their room and learned why he'd wanted the berries.

chapter 13

The room smelled of rebellion.

The dog sat on Petros's bed, watching Zola.

Zola didn't hear Petros coming. He nearly tipped over the ink bottle. "Shah! Don't you know to make a little noise when you come in?"

Zola had mashed the berries. He dipped his pen in the juice and wrote. Petros said, "Why not just use ink?"

"Did you see the stains on Lambros's fingers? Mulberry juice. The fruit sustained him. This ink is symbolic."

Petros rolled his eyes. A romantic, Mama said, when his brother got like this. Petros asked, "What will you do with it?"

"I can print secret messages," Zola said.

This sounded interesting. However, Petros didn't want to say so. He sat down on the end of his bed, where Zola's dog shouldn't have been. Both were patient as Zola wrote a word, dipped his pen, and wrote another.

Zola looked at Petros from the corner of his eye. "The berries don't make as much juice as I thought."

Petros ignored that. Zola had found some clean white

paper that looked very good with mulberry juice on it. "Where did you get such paper?"

Zola held out the finished product. It said *Germans lose battle to British in North Africa.* The dog looked impressed, but Petros said, "Everyone knows this already."

"Already people want war news," Zola said. "We can tell it." .

"We don't listen to the radio anymore," Petros pointed out.

"Papa will, once the Germans set up camp and settle in like the Italians," Zola said, going back to writing as he talked. "He hid the radio, he didn't bury it. Besides, this is only the first message."

Petros didn't care for Zola's know-it-all tone. "Even a first message should tell people something they don't already know," he said. "The war could be over before we can have the radio back."

"Will a man ask his neighbor on one side, who's a German sympathizer, what he's heard?" Zola asked him. "Or will he go to the neighbor on his other side, the one who's only hungry? The one who might lie to the German soldiers in return for a meal?"

Petros said nothing. Surely neighbors could be trusted.

Zola sighed in a world-weary way. "People talked last month. They disagreed but still they spoke up. This month neighbors are divided by those words. Each disagreement is a gate locked against them."

This kind of talk troubled Petros. He couldn't help thinking of Elia's father. But then he thought of Grandfather

Lemos, who never agreed with Elia's father either, and yet they lived in the same house.

Petros said, "Still, people talk to each other."

"People used to talk. Now they whisper. They read notes," Zola said. He appeared to grow bored. "Aren't you supposed to be going to sleep?"

Petros didn't like Zola's tone. "You can't leave all this in the house," he said, waving a hand over the ink and notes. "If Mama finds it, I'll get blamed too."

Zola got up fast and knocked Petros back onto his bed. The dog jumped off. "You're not to say one word to anyone," Zola whispered fiercely. "Do you hear?"

Petros pulled his legs up hard, thumping Zola in the ribs with his knees. Zola leaped away.

"Just be quiet," he said.

Petros got under the sheet. If Zola needed more mulberries, he would have to climb the tree and get them himself.

chapter 14

By the next morning, Zola had printed his messages.

He stepped up on the end of Petros's bed over and over, until Petros woke from a dream of earthquakes. He got up to avoid being stepped on.

Outside, the sky was a deep purple. The only dim light in the room came from the desk lamp, covered with a towel. The birds were trying out a few peeps before beginning the morning song.

Zola was hiding his notes on the upper shelves, moving two at a time. He could leave them to dry there while the morning's work was done. "They dry slowly," he said.

Petros came to life.

He saw a great many pieces of that white paper strewn around on the desk and a low bookcase that now held only a few books. Again, Petros wondered where Zola had gotten such excellent paper.

"Once the Germans come, you and Elia can help," Zola offered graciously. "I'm going to need a lot of mulberries."

It was on the tip of Petros's tongue to tell his brother to take a big bucket, but he saw the notes looked like a young child had written them very neatly. He said, "These look strange."

The wording remained the same: *Germans lose battle to British in North Africa.* Not exactly news. But so many notes looked like a secret. An important secret. This might be the best sport Zola had ever suggested.

"I must make the lettering plain, very plain," Zola said, "so the soldiers can't ask me to write something and say, see, these letters are written by the same hand."

Petros nodded, although he didn't care for the sound of anyone guessing Zola had written these notes. He handed them up to Zola, who stood on the bed. "How will you deliver them?"

"Carefully," Zola said in a self-important way. "Enemies are everywhere."

This was true. Even now, the enemy of these notes slept just down the hall. "So. In secret, then?" Petros said, as if there were ever any doubt.

"Yes. I'll go this afternoon when everyone is napping."

Petros tried to look like he was thinking very hard. "Perhaps Elia and I should deliver them. Perhaps Stavros."

"Why is that?"

"Soldiers won't pay any attention to us. We're only boys."

This reasoning could have tipped the scale either way. Petros saw it on Zola's face. "It protects you, Zola," Petros hurried to say. "What if you got arrested?"

"If you get arrested, Mama will kill me. And I'll kill you."

"So we won't get arrested," Petros said, closing the deal.

* * *

Petros ate his breakfast of bread and olives quickly, eager to get on to his garden. It wasn't long before he spotted Elia working across the road. He ran over and arranged for Elia to meet him at the well when the Lemos family lay down for a nap.

"What are we doing?" Elia wanted to know.

"Something dangerous," Petros said. Elia's eyes lit up as if he'd said, *Something fun.*

People carrying their belongings continued to pass the house throughout the morning and made Petros feel a little sick. Perhaps anyone who *could* was leaving. Those who didn't have good farms or sure businesses and were often hungry figured things would only get worse.

After the midday meal, Mama lay down for a nap. Sophie read a book. Papa and Old Mario sat on the porch smoking, and Zola joined them.

Petros met Elia at the well and told him what Zola had in mind. Elia said, "Why do we need Stavros?"

"We'll make it look like a game. Someone watching will be interested in the boy throwing, or the boy catching. Who'll see the third boy drop a piece of paper?"

Zola peeked around the corner of the house and waved them over. Elia ambled over to Zola, making it clear that he wasn't going to be bossed around.

Zola waved a harder *come on.* "Are you ready?" he whispered impatiently when the boys stood in front of him.

Zola's printed messages were wadded to make tight little

balls. A folded piece of paper might tempt the wrong people to pick it up—what proud soldier would pick up a piece of wadded paper out of mere curiosity?

On the way to town, Elia and Petros decided Zola's plan was excellent. They agreed not to tell him they thought so.

Petros expected Stavros to pretend a lack of interest at first. Instead, Stavros acted like he'd been in charge all along and made them practice. They stood in the corners of his room, tossing a small cloth bag of sand around as they chanted, "Throw, catch, drop."

Auntie looked in once, saw boys playing ball, and asked them no questions. In only a few minutes they got the rhythm of it down. Each one of them put notes in his pockets and left the house.

Italian soldiers were everywhere in clusters, more than ever before. Lounging on doorsteps. Having a coffee at an open café. Strolling. All around the soldiers, the village moved on in its usual way.

A boy only a little older than Zola stood at a windowsill, flirting with a girl. Old men played cards at a table in a garden. Women bustled from shop to shop, carrying boxes of paper money, their fingers hooked under the heavy twine. There were soldiers in the village, but everyone had learned to live with this.

Elia, Stavros, and Petros ran through the village, calling to each other, tossing the sand ball back and forth. Boys at play didn't look disciplined. Hot, and panting whenever they stopped moving for a moment, how could they hold secrets? The soldiers hardly noticed them, and after a few throws, the boys relaxed.

They ran into yards and into doorways where they shouldn't go. Once, a soldier caught the sand ball, then threw it onward to Stavros. With the soldier's easy smile upon them, war seemed only a game everyone was playing.

Zola had fallen asleep on the veranda, and they found him there when they got back home. Papa and Old Mario had already gone back to work. "Be careful," Zola said after they described their adventure. "The Germans are playing to win."

Petros knew how to read his brother. He agreed with Stavros and Elia. It had gone well. But Elia said, "We're careful and smart."

"You have to be both," Zola said, frowning. "You have to be everything but too sure of yourself."

At bedtime, Zola sat in the darkness, waiting for the household to sleep. He planned to write his next message.

Petros asked, "What will you write?"

"You'll see tomorrow," Zola said.

Petros rolled onto his side, glad he, at least, could sleep through the night. Also, Petros knew Zola would soon talk about anything he did well.

"I might deliver these messages myself," Zola said.

Petros pretended to be asleep for a few moments before he really was.

chapter 15

Petros woke with one thought already in mind. *The Germans haven't come.* He knew this was best for everyone, and yet it was as if he, having tripped over a rake, was still waiting to fall.

His next thought had to do with Zola's notes. He wanted to play this game with Elia and Stavros again. He was brave and he was bold—that felt good. More, he'd put a proud gleam in his brother's eyes.

Zola'd dragged himself off his pillow as Petros sat up. Already the skin between Zola's eyebrows looked knotted with a fight between the desire to keep the secret of his new message and the need to tell it.

"I guess you want to know what I wrote." Sleep slurred the words.

Petros did, but it was necessary not to look too eager. He headed out of the room. "Food first."

In the kitchen, Sophie asked, "Why are the Germans taking so long?"

Mama made the usual annoyed click of her tongue. "You're impatient for them to get here?"

"It's only because this waiting is so hard."

"Be glad we don't live in a city like Athens or a port like Piraeus, or even too close to the railways," Mama said to her. It was said in the village that the Germans took those cities first.

"Then why do they come at all? Why not stay there?"

"The mountains," Mama said. "The Germans want Lambros and the soldiers like him to be cut off from food and medicine."

"If that's true," Sophie said, "Lambros and the others should have stayed home and done nothing."

"The Germans would still be in Athens and Piraeus," Mama said as if the subject tired her. "An army must be dealt with."

Petros understood the war to be something large and rolling toward them like an avalanche. Something they could do nothing about. But it made so little noise, he could sometimes forget it was coming.

At breakfast Papa told Zola he could no longer walk about town alone. He'd grown tall very fast, taller than Papa. He'd grown some pale down on his chin that made him look even more grown-up.

"Let me use your razor," Zola said.

Papa said, "You'll still be tall." Zola stormed out of the house and to his work in the garden, his dog trotting worriedly behind.

Petros worked all morning to clear a bit more of his land. He put in several more pepper plants. When someone called his name, he looked up to see Mr. Katzen, who bought cheese and eggs from Mama, waving his cane. "You've lost a pepper plant. Do you see?"

Petros looked where Mr. Katzen pointed. The pepper plant was nearly covered by the weeds he'd pulled. "I stepped on it and the top broke off."

"So that's it? You won't plant it?"

Petros picked up the pepper plant and his hand rake and dug a hole for it. What did it matter?

"Don't give up on it, Petros," Mr. Katzen said. "Not just because it's a little bit crippled."

"Are you leaving?" Petros asked.

"Leaving for where?"

"The Germans are coming."

"I've heard," Mr. Katzen said. "But there's nowhere left to go."

"To one of the islands," Petros suggested. "To Crete."

Mr. Katzen shook his head. "I already live in the hills. I'm too old to start living somewhere else." He sounded like Papa. Petros guessed he was too old for the German army to bother with anyway.

When the morning's work was done, Zola stopped to talk to Petros before going on to the house. "This next message is excellent."

Petros didn't rise to the bait.

"I've said we must lock arms to stand against the wind," Zola added.

This was the note they would take such trouble for? "Don't you have anything better to say?"

"It's a more careful note," Zola said.

"It doesn't mean anything."

"The wind is on its way to Crete," Zola said. "It was on the radio before Lambros came home. Didn't you understand what they were saying?"

A fresh stubborn anger rose in Petros. "Surely there are a few things you don't understand," he said to Zola. "If you knew everything, you would have been the fellow speaking to us from Cairo."

Zola sighed heavily, as if to say, *Well, of course not everything. But this much!* "It all comes down to the canal," he said.

"The Suez Canal," Petros said, to show he'd listened to the news.

"The British control the canal. If the Germans could fight from Crete, they could overcome the British."

"So it all comes down to Crete," Petros said. "The Germans want to go there."

"Everyone goes there," Zola said.

Petros wanted to burst Zola's self-important bubble. "It's the only way out of here now."

"Isn't that what I said?"

"Why don't you put that in the note?"

Zola smacked his forehead, making a little show of rolling his eyes. "Because everyone knows that already."

chapter 16

At the midday meal, Petros swallowed a boiled egg, hardly bothering to chew. Old Mario put two eggs on his own plate.

Petros slowed down to fill up on macaroni with olive oil and garlic. The others ate zucchini and beans and tomatoes with this, but Petros was tired of eating vegetables.

Then, as the meal was nearly finished, the murmur of something like rocks falling could be heard in the distance. The family put down their forks as one, listening.

"Trucks," Old Mario said, and Petros swallowed his last bite whole.

Papa said, "Old Mario, go up to the roof and count them. See if they all go to the village. Everyone else remain at the table." He went to the front of the house, and from there, outside.

Mama sat just long enough to make up her mind to go with Papa.

Zola was right behind Mama as she left the kitchen.

Petros dashed out the back door. He eyed the bushes critically. The gravel looked fresh to his eyes, but it covered all the signs of digging. A few of the smaller flowering plants still looked a bit wilted, but only a gardener might notice the roots had been disturbed.

At the corner of the house, Petros stopped and concentrated on what he'd really come to see. A jeep was stopped in the road. Trucks rumbled past, going toward the village, raising dust.

Papa stood at the gate, Mama and Zola right behind him, facing two soldiers. A few more stood at the ready in the road. The soldiers looked exactly as Zola had told him they would, as Lambros had described them. Their faces set as if carved in stone. Bodies so upright they appeared to be tall, even though neither one was taller than Zola.

They started for the house. Petros froze, watching, but in his head, he screamed. If the Germans searched the house, they'd find the notes drying on the shelf over his bed. All that Papa had done to save them would be lost.

Papa argued and shook his head no. They brushed past him, stiff with importance. Petros felt as if his arms and legs had filled with sand, but he turned and ran clumsily back to the kitchen.

Ignoring Sophie's shrill scolding, he snatched up Mama's scrap bucket. He heard the soldiers' boots on the veranda, and then in the parlor, as he ran to the room he shared with Zola. If his arms and legs were filled with sand, it drained from his fingers and the bottoms of his feet with each step.

Petros scrambled onto his bed, reaching high to scoop up

the notes into the bucket. Several of them floated to the floor. He made sure the shelf was clean, then climbed down to capture the rest of the slippery notes.

In the parlor, someone spoke in a harsh tone, and then another voice followed like a shadow, saying everything again in Greek because Papa and Zola both pretended not to understand German.

Petros was only grateful this conversation took so long. Some of the notes had floated under the bed.

"Some of this furniture must be removed. The commander needs this room."

"Someone sleeps here." A lie.

Petros nodded. Sometimes a lie was necessary.

The shadow followed more closely on the harsh voice, saying, "Whoever sleeps here can use another room. The commander will bring his own bed."

Papa said nothing. Someone moved around the parlor, wooden boot heels loud on the floor.

Petros dropped the last note into the bucket. Remembering the way Papa had reacted when Zola suggested hanging a flag, he lifted Zola's mattress and yanked the paper flag out from under it.

His hands shook as he rolled it up and threw the rolled paper out the bedroom window like a spear, where it would fall into the bushes at the side of the house. This war was no longer a game—Petros saw that now.

Petros grabbed the bucket and peeked out to see Sophie

standing just outside the parlor. Without looking his way, she motioned with her hand to hurry him.

Petros ran toward her quietly.

"Your family will stay and tend your farm. Your wife will cook. Is this understood?"

"Yes."

"Yes, sir," the shadow said, and Papa echoed, "Yes, sir."

One soldier—Petros realized he was an officer—was pointing to things around the room. "These chairs, the sofa, put them outside. A truck will come for them. Empty this chest. We'll take that table."

His mother made a small sound.

"I don't understand why this matters," Papa said, reminding Mama there was nothing of any importance but their lives. The hard voice didn't reply, but the shadow spoke.

"We need them at the command post," the officer said, and Mama gripped Papa's arm. But Papa nodded and the officer said, "Put everything on the veranda before morning." He turned away, reading the list in the shadow's hands.

Petros hurried into the kitchen, where he stopped to scrape his plate over the notes in the bucket. Sophie followed him, whispering, "What are you doing?"

A soldier stepped into the back doorway, a dark form blocking the sunlight. "What do you do here?" he said in poor Greek. Something inside Petros stood still. Even his hands forgot to shake.

"For the pig." Petros was glad his father and brother and

Old Mario ate as if they were in a race. Their plates looked as if he'd already scraped them. The soldier didn't look closely at the bucket. Sophie stood against the wall, watching, as Petros scraped her plate clean and Zola's.

The soldier crossed the kitchen and started down the hall toward the bedrooms.

Petros left the bucket and ran outside, heading for the other end of the house. He pushed his way behind the bushes, looking for the rolled paper flag. At the sound of voices in the room above, he dropped to a squat under the thickest bush. He sat still, even when the shutters flew open over his head.

The officer gave orders Petros didn't understand. He moved to the corner of the house and saw the doors to the balcony off Mama's room thrown open. Papa was right—the Germans were looking all through the house. Petros ran quickly to hide in the shadows of the arbor.

From the goat pen, Fifi saw him and bleated.

He stopped at the far end of the arbor, gripped one of the rocks at the base, and pulled against it with all his weight. The rock slid out and dropped heavily to the ground. Petros brushed his hand around inside the cavity to be sure it was dry. He found a few jars of mulberry juice that Zola had secreted there.

Each summer he and Zola picked several bunches of grapes and hid them here. Once hidden in the cool, dark hollow, the grapes lasted and could be enjoyed long after the crop had been crushed for wine or dried for raisins. It was the best hiding place they had. Petros angled the flag into the narrow space.

It was a struggle to get the rock back into place. Petros finally sat down and pushed with both feet. He felt great satisfaction, hearing a last scrape as it settled in. He would tell Zola later on, when they met in their room, and his brother would be pleased.

The crunch of boots on the gravel warned Petros of a soldier close by. His stomach tightened, his breath caught. He didn't want to be found here, questioned. But his arms and legs were no longer made of sand. Excitement thrummed in his veins.

The soldier gave a shout.

chapter 17

Petros gathered his feet under him but didn't try to run. He knew the names of some things in German and felt certain the German had shouted something about the truck, Papa's truck.

He hid while the first German was joined by another, along with Papa, who told them he used the truck to take his vegetables to market. He told them twice, because the interpreter had stayed at the house and the soldiers didn't understand. All of them walked back as Papa repeated his remarks about the truck.

Petros stayed there under the arbor, thinking about the soldiers and their tone of voice, hard and cold. Papa made his voice not afraid exactly, but hesitant as he pretended not to understand the soldiers, either.

Petros knew Papa felt small facing the soldiers and their cold manner. It bothered him. Papa could be as bossy as the soldiers, but his voice never made Petros feel small.

He heard the jeep start. Petros got up, reaching the driveway in time to see the Germans leaving, five of them looking straight ahead like the tiny carved figures in the toy trucks he'd buried.

Sophie, Mama, and Papa were all on the veranda. He could hear their voices. Zola was just coming into the kitchen as Petros stepped in through the back. "Did you take my notes?" Zola whispered.

Petros saw the awful white of his brother's face and knew he was scared. He lifted the scraps bucket.

Zola snatched the bucket away, his fright turning suddenly into anger. Petros could hardly believe it and would have said so, only everyone started coming inside and the moment to fight was gone. Old Mario, coming from the roof, was shouting curses on the German army as he reached the bottom of the stairs.

"How can we live with a stranger in the house?" Mama clapped a hand to her forehead. "A German officer!"

"Papa, we are—" Zola was shouting. Whatever else he said couldn't be understood through everyone else's voices, but Petros gathered it had to do with going into town.

"Enough!" Papa said with a fast motion of his hands that suggested parting the waves. Mama crossed her arms.

Old Mario said, "Soldiers stopped at Lemos's house at the same time. There were four trucks that drove on, then another, five in all. One remains down the road at Omeros's."

"I want to phone Lemos," Papa said, speaking of Elia's grandfather.

"Be careful what you say," Old Mario said. "Someone may be listening in from Omeros's house."

Many times Mama believed the Omeros grandmother

listened in on the party line, hoping to hear gossip. Lately Papa worried that gossip wasn't all she listened for.

Papa said, "We'll say only the things everyone else is saying. Then we make the parlor ready." He picked up the telephone to dial.

Mama moved to the sink to wash dishes, working noisily, roughly.

Papa said to Lemos, "Are you well?" and then listened.

Sophie tried to look into the scraps bucket. Zola yanked it away. But it was Petros he punched in the shoulder. "Don't you know better than to touch my things?" he whispered fiercely.

Petros ignored the hit. "Would you rather the soldiers touched them?" he said.

"You." Sophie poked Petros with a sharp fingernail. "What were you up to?"

Zola answered for him. "Nothing."

"No fighting," Mama said. "Make yourselves useful."

"I'm feeding the pig," Zola said. He strode out, slamming the bucket against the doorway. Mama shouted at him, but Papa hissed at her to be quiet, and Zola was forgotten.

Petros stood rigid and swore to himself he would never tell where he'd hidden the paper flag. Zola could twist his arm and bend his little finger back, and Petros would never tell.

Papa said, "Good." He hung up and asked Mama, "Now what is it?"

Mama shrugged. "Boys."

"I think we're the only ones to be honored with a house-guest," Papa said heavily. He and Mama headed for the parlor.

Old Mario and Petros and Sophie followed them.

"Lemos's wife is badly upset," Papa said. "Her dining room, their bed. At least we have our bed."

Old Mario nodded, but Mama sat down hard on the sofa that would be gone soon. She leaned like someone who'd been standing a long time in a strong wind. "What will we do?"

"We'll put the furniture they want out on the veranda," Papa said as Zola came back inside. Zola was put right to work.

No one could sleep that afternoon.

Elia came over to Petros's house to escape his grand-mother's complaints. "Let's play marbles next to your well."

They'd no sooner begun than Stavros showed up. "Auntie's spending her afternoon in the church," he said. "It's cool in there, but I'm surrounded by grandmothers."

They each tried to win the game. But they also shouted en-couragement to each other as they'd never done. All at once Mama stood over them. "What's this?" she asked, scooping up the glass marble.

Elia was flushed with the happiness of winning. "Petros's shooter."

Petros groaned. Mama turned a warrior's eye on him. "Where's a switch? I'll beat all of you and feed you to the pig. Where was this?"

Elia looked an apology at Petros. "In my pouch," Petros said. Where he hadn't given it one thought.

"This came from Spiro?" Mama asked. "Are there more?"

"No."

Mama turned, her arm coming up, and the boys screamed, "No!"

She threw the marble into the well. Stavros dropped to the ground in despair.

"You couldn't keep it," Mama said in a loud whisper, as if the Germans had already arrived. She left the boys slumped down beside the well.

Petros felt drained somehow, made flat, like something run over on the road. He and Elia dropped to sit beside Stavros, all of them with their backs against the well.

"I should have said it was mine," Elia said.

"No, you should have said it was *mine*," Stavros told him, and they laughed.

chapter 18

Later in the day, Papa sent Petros and Zola to clean the chicken house. This was hot, smelly work that disturbed the chickens. They flapped and squawked and made a trundling run or two at the boys' ankles before escaping outside.

At first Petros and Zola didn't speak, only scraped their shovels across the floor and sweated. The chill of fear was fading fast. Their bellies were full, and the Germans gone. No one hurt. Perhaps things weren't so bad after all.

As the minutes wore on and Zola didn't trouble him, Petros thought Zola now realized he'd been right to throw the notes into the bucket. He'd no sooner decided this was true than Zola said, "The notes we fed to the pig don't matter. We must send out a more urgent message now."

"Look for the other nests," Petros said, because several of Mama's chickens persisted in setting up housekeeping *under* the henhouse.

"Being commander is a big responsibility," Zola said. He stopped working and leaned on his shovel.

Petros could see how this was going to go. His brother had

done nothing to help when the Germans came and now acted as if he hadn't gotten angry that Petros had. He thought enough time had passed that the whole matter would be forgotten.

It wouldn't be forgotten—Petros promised himself that much.

Zola said, "He'll go out each day like a man of business, I think."

Petros stopped scraping and sat on his heels, leaning against the wall. He was in the mood to torture his brother just a little. "What if he searches our room?"

Zola looked at Petros from the corner of his eye. "There will be nothing for him to find."

Petros thought this was Zola's way of asking what he'd done with the flag. But he wasn't ready to tell. He wouldn't *be* ready until Zola was prepared to be grateful. "So no more notes?"

"The Germans are big," Zola said. "We are small. We must be small and smart. Lambros said this to Papa."

Again, Petros wished he'd gone inside to hear Lambros. He forgot about torturing Zola. "What are you planning?"

"To send a different message," Zola said, sweeping his shovel across the floor, coming close enough to Petros to bump his sandal.

Petros ignored this. "What news do we have?"

Zola said, "Victory for Greece. For Lambros."

Petros shot to his feet. "What have you heard?"

"Nothing, nothing," Zola said with a wave of his hand. "But it's a cheering message, isn't it? So if it's more than a month until we can send another message, people's spirits are stronger."

"I suppose." Petros wished his brother would be a little more careful of his spirits, which were now somewhat lowered.

"Such good news will make everyone more hopeful," Zola said.

Petros allowed himself to be convinced. It gave him a thrill to think of running through the village again.

That night, as before, Zola worked when everyone else slept. He waited until he heard Papa snoring before he lit a candle to work by. Petros woke to the scratch of the match, the unexpectedly sharp light from the candle, and the rustling of paper.

Zola worked carefully to avoid stains on his fingers or clothing. When he pulled the little bar on the pen, it sucked up just the right amount of juice and no more. The spills on the sheet of stiff brown paper covering his desk came from setting the pen down when he needed to stretch. Petros's eyelids drooped.

"I worked in the garden this morning," Zola said, waking Petros again. "And worked through the entire afternoon without resting."

Petros pulled his sheet over his head.

"While you're sleeping, I'm printing."

Petros pushed the sheet down. "When will you be done?"

"When I am, that's all," Zola said, and then relented. "Tonight. I'll finish tonight. Then we must watch for a chance. You'll wait till Mama sends you to town."

As he wrote, Zola blew on the paper, helping the juice dry.

"Good." Petros thought he might care more in the morning, but for now, sleep came to him with the breeze coming through the window, smelling of lemon balm and lavender and thyme.

Zola spoke directly into his ear, waking him.

"I've been thinking," Zola said. He enjoyed a good plan, and he liked Petros to know when he'd planned well. "You should pick the last of the mulberries. We need enough ink to last us until next year's mulberries. For now that we've begun this way, no one will trust a message written in pencil or black ink."

"Probably they don't care."

"They will," Zola said. "My messages are the ones they'll take notice of."

Petros turned away from Zola's voice.

"You shouldn't get juice on your fingers," Zola said, pushing at Petros's shoulder. "In case the notes are found by the Germans, none of us must have stains."

Petros narrowed his eyes and thought it might be pleasant to eat the rest of the berries Zola wanted, they were so ripe. It might be said making ink of the sweetest berries was a terrible waste.

This never crossed Zola's note-writing mind. Nothing else mattered—Petros smiled a little. Perhaps Zola hadn't realized his flag was gone after all.

If he'd noticed, he wouldn't be bothering Petros about mulberries. The bed jiggled as Zola bumped it, moving away. Petros almost fell back to sleep happy.

But then a worry settled heavily on his shoulders. If they made more ink, Zola would have to hide it somewhere. Under the arbor, in the space between the rocks, where he already had some hidden, was the likeliest place.

chapter 19

Early the next morning, Petros woke up as Zola wadded up his messages, rolled them in his palms until they were smaller than clay marbles, and stuffed them into his pockets. "This way . . . ," he said, but didn't finish.

The arbor wasn't an easy place to visit secretly in the middle of the day. It was too easy for Sophie or Mama to look out a window and know a boy was up to something. More than that, it wouldn't be easy to hide the flag in another such excellent place.

Zola sat, then fell into his bed as if it swallowed him up. He didn't even move to make himself more comfortable. Petros waited five minutes more, until Zola was sleeping deeply, before feeling his way through the dark hall and kitchen, carrying his sandals. He put them on after he'd crossed the veranda.

There was no morning light, but the inky darkness of night had given way to a strange purple color in the air. Petros plucked the flag from its hiding place. He hurried to let himself into the pump house, careful not to wake Old Mario, who slept nearby. Petros wrapped the roll of paper in a scrap of oilcloth he found in a pile of useful things.

Climbing the rough shelves in the pump house, Petros placed the flag at the top. Anyone who looked there would pay the oilcloth no attention at all. He got only one small splinter for his trouble.

He went back to the kitchen for the key to the padlock on the gate, then unwound the chain. The sun was coming up as he crossed the road, heading to Elia's. Behind him, Old Mario's door creaked open.

Petros tossed a pebble at Elia's window to rouse him. When Elia looked out, Petros beckoned and crept away again, to wait for him at the road. A truck passed, filled with soldiers.

Elia came out his back door.

"We must pick as many of the mulberries as we can," Petros said, "and we must keep our hands clean."

Elia nodded, catching on. He said, "Use the mulberry leaves like a potholder, pick the fruit, and drop it into the bucket without touching it."

Soon the smell of coffee wafted on the air, making their bellies grumble. Old Mario crossed the yard to feed the goats. Fifi got loose and trotted over to stand below the tree. The boys picked a bucketful of berries before their mamas began to wonder where they were.

Only a bucketful, because the leaves made them clumsy. Even without trying, they dropped enough berries to keep Fifi contented. She ate a leaf as happily as a berry. The only trouble came when Petros had to put her back into the pen, and then tie the rope to her collar once more. He got many bites.

Going into the kitchen, he heard Mama say, "He treats that animal like a dog."

"A good farmer keeps his animals content," Papa said as he dipped a crust of bread into his coffee. Petros let his chest swell just the littlest bit. He did keep Fifi content.

German troop trucks rumbled past the house while the family was still at breakfast. The family hurried to the front windows.

"Men and supplies," Papa said. Officers rode between some of the trucks in jeeps. Everyone drew a breath in relief whenever a jeep didn't stop at their gate. Then came the realization: the German army had come to Amphissa. Petros glanced at Zola, who pulled a wadded note out of his pocket to show Petros, shoved it back down.

"Some of these trucks must be going straight through," Papa said.

"Through to where?" This was Sophie.

Papa said, "Perhaps to the railroad. Or to follow the coast around to the Corinth Canal. To get to Crete."

Papa and Old Mario agreed the commander would settle his men in the village before they'd see him. They still had their house to themselves and were free to speak as they pleased. Yet they lowered their voices to speak of the commander.

They stopped counting the trucks that passed by. It was more like they'd decided not to look.

During the day, people came to the gate to sell things. Villagers, leaving Amphissa for any place more hospitable than their home had just become. Papa said the boys weren't to open the gate.

Mama was lucky to buy a pair of shoes for Zola, who'd outgrown his work boots. This pair had been worn but didn't have any holes. The shoes were taken out of a feed sack, and money stuffed to fill it.

Mostly Mama shook her head—she wanted nothing but shoes, even if they were too big for Zola right then. No one was making shoes. But she often gave away a cabbage and a couple of potatoes, because she didn't like people to go empty-handed.

Only a day later, it became more difficult. People didn't want money. They needed eggs and cheese. They were glad to get bread. It was widely agreed the Basilis sisters were selling cardboard disguised as bread. For a pair of boots for Papa, worn and very dirty, Mama gave up a young chicken and felt she'd made an even trade.

Papa looked at the boots and said, "I hope it was an old chicken."

"These boots will last longer than the chicken," she said back to Papa. "They just aren't as pretty."

Papa and Old Mario strung goat bells on a rope all along the top of the rock wall. The wall was shoulder-high to Papa, but a man could climb over it. Now one touch on the rope set the whole place to ringing.

chapter 20

The next afternoon, Petros, Elia, and Stavros worked again as a team. Right away, they saw how much the village was changed.

There were only a few Germans to be seen, sitting in trucks or standing in the school building doorways. But the village was in hiding. Old men didn't sit in their gardens. Gates were closed, shutters pulled tight at windows.

Petros, Elia, and Stavros threw the sand ball as before, dropping notes into boots left at the edge of the garden, the chair beside a door, a window box. They scrambled up and down a short flight of steps and dropped a note into a flowerpot. Their voices rang shrill with nerves.

Twice Elia missed the ball, throwing off the rhythm. The first time the game halted for a split second, as Petros stopped cold in shock. Then Stavros laughed in a loud jeering way. Elia jeered back.

They looked like they were fighting among themselves. If they drew any attention, none of it would be curiosity. Petros wished Zola had seen how quickly Stavros saved the moment.

And how quickly Elia understood. He threw the ball to Petros and the game went on.

Only one message was left on a gravel walk as if the paper had fallen out of their pockets. This was when Stavros ran around a corner and nearly slammed into a German soldier.

Stavros halted just in time but remained there, stock-still, head down. Petros and Elia stopped too, panting from the running, uncertain what to do. This soldier looked young, but hardened somehow. The Italians were rowdy in comparison, either joking or full of temper.

It was then Petros realized there were no Italians on the streets. Not a single one. The Italians were on the German side in this war. Where had those soldiers gone?

Stavros stepped back, still looking at the ground, so the soldier could walk on. When he did, Stavros walked a few steps away from the young soldier before he skipped a step or two. Petros saw the note drop.

Stavros ran on as if this foolish bravery didn't risk all their lives.

Petros wanted to hit him but he also enjoyed his cousin's foolish courage. Love and pride ran fast through veins, faster by far than blood, Petros discovered, laughing with the thrill of it.

"Ya ha rah," Stavros shouted, his voice strong and deep. Petros threw him the sand ball.

Stavros caught it and tossed it to Elia, who didn't miss as Petros flicked a note through the iron fencing of a garden. An old man stepped out from his veranda, giving Petros a fright. It could just as easily have been a soldier he hadn't noticed.

The old man bent at the waist to put his cigarette out. Petros thought he grabbed the note as he straightened up. Zola was right, he realized. People had taken notice of these messages. But he pushed the thought away, catching the sand ball and tossing it to Stavros.

When they were done, and sitting on a curbstone like boys who'd grown tired of a game, Petros said to Stavros in a low voice, "Where are the Italians?"

"Gone," Stavros said. "The Germans sent them away. All in one night. They were gone by morning. I saw it."

Elia said, "Papa heard a rumor the Germans killed them. Shot them dead in the road."

Stavros nodded.

Petros said, "That can't be true. The Germans and the Italians are on the same side."

Stavros said, "I asked my grandmother what she thought of this. She told me that in a fight with the Italians, there are rumors. In a fight with the Germans, there are only losses."

Petros and Elia both sat back slightly. Petros felt a chill between his shoulder blades—this was why *he* sat back.

Stavros shrugged. "She's only an old grandmother talking."

The boys sat silent. That Stavros would attempt to make less of Auntie's opinion gave that much more weight to it. Together they watched the women hurrying through the marketplace, carrying eggs or tomatoes in boxes, or chickens in cages.

Some old women were bent double with the weight of their produce. None of them smiled or talked to each other as they had done when the Italian soldiers were here.

"We weren't so afraid of the Italians," Stavros said. "Their eyes told us always where we stood. That one's eyes told me nothing."

Petros didn't need to ask whom Stavros meant by *that one*. It was very unlike Stavros to say he'd been frightened, even for a heartbeat.

When Petros got home, he found Zola weeding near the gate so he could stop there, away from everyone else. "It was different this time," Petros said, crushing a weed under his shoe.

"Different?"

"The Italians are gone."

Zola didn't look impressed. "So it's the Germans instead."

"They're our enemy."

"We're at war."

"Differently," Petros said. "They didn't stop us, but they didn't smile at the game either. These soldiers talk to no one but among themselves."

Zola said nothing. Petros left him there, but later, in their room, he said, "I think you were wise to send this message out now. But when the commander comes—"

"We'll use our wits," Zola said.

The words Petros needed hadn't come to him. "This is serious business we're up to," he said.

"We must do our part," Zola whispered. "This is for the war effort."

"Those are only words you've heard on the radio," Petros said. "Papa's put the radio in the cellar. Perhaps we should stop."

"Stop what?" Papa said, stepping inside their room. The room got so quiet Petros thought Papa was the only one still breathing.

"Talking about the radio," Zola said in a way that nearly fooled Petros into believing him.

"The Germans are here," Papa said, looking hard at Zola. "Ours is the only battle that matters now."

Zola said, "Yes, Papa."

Papa went on down the hall to his bedroom. Petros steeled himself for the sneering look he expected from Zola, a look that meant little brothers were as easily frightened as mice. But in Zola's eyes there was only determination.

"History is being made all around us," Zola said in a whisper because they didn't hear Papa's door close. "Don't you want to be part of history?"

"I want to be part of the future."

"That too," Zola said. "What good is history if you aren't around to enjoy it?"

"Exactly," Petros said. "We must remember the danger."

"That you must," Zola said, and then he grinned. "Papa will kill us if you get caught."

"He'll kill you first," Petros said, "because you're older and should know better."

chapter 21

The next morning, Mama sent Petros out to pick the zucchini. He didn't like to do it. These plants spread their stems like the arms on an octopus, and the prickly vines made itchy work for him. But he was there to see Papa and Elia's father going down the road toward the village.

Elia came across the road. "Your father offered to trade your farm for ours."

"That wouldn't be fair," Petros said, and then looked away when Elia's face flushed red.

He didn't mean to hurt Elia, but it was true. The Lemos family's farm, while a fine one, was small. Their mules wouldn't be employed for enough weeks to make it pay to feed them if Papa didn't lease them several times a year to plow his fields.

"They want the commander to stay here because your farm has plenty of vegetables in the garden," Elia said.

"You have lots of vegetables," Petros said. He regretted saying the Lemos farm was small. He wished his brother had remained near enough to weigh in on this matter. Behind

Elia, so far off they swam in a sea of green, Zola moved alongside Old Mario in the wheat field.

Elia wore a small mean look on his face. "You have the bigger parlor. That's what my mother said. He'll sleep in your parlor."

Petros sensed a distance opening up between them. He'd known Elia his whole life without knowing this feeling. He got the oddest sort of ache around his heart. "Papa wouldn't trade this farm."

"Your father wants you and Zola and Sophie to be safe. But my grandfather said no one will be safe with him there."

Him. The commander, of course. A figure more terrifying in Petros's imagination day by day. "We didn't invite him."

"Mama says we'll be safe," Elia said. "We have nothing to hide."

This had the awful ring of truth. Elia's family had no Americans and no soldiers. Elia's father buried their gun and anything else they were afraid to lose, but not every book or plate they had with an English name on it. His family spoke only Greek because Greek was their only language. It struck Petros suddenly that Elia was taking a great chance with his family's safety.

Stavros's family had the difficulty of protecting Lambros, and Petros's family had the danger of being Americans, but Elia's family had nothing that put them at risk.

Except Elia.

And Petros and Zola, who had involved him in a dangerous game.

"Your father said the trade would stand when the war was over," Elia said. "My father was for it, but my grandfather said no. He didn't want to live with a high officer of the German army. Not even to own a farm twice the size."

Elia spoke as if he hadn't been angry moments ago. As if this were simply a matter of interest to both of them. Petros and Elia had always been close. Most of the time Petros preferred the prick of Elia's quick hurtful words to the burn of Stavros's long-held grudges.

But with the other boys, even Stavros, Petros had always been made to feel a little apart. It was hard to forgive Elia for making him feel that way now, even for a few minutes.

Petros carried the basket of zucchini past him. "I have to feed the chickens," he said. This wasn't strictly true, but chickens could always eat, and he didn't want to talk to Elia anymore.

Elia said, "We could walk into the village and get Stavros's thinking on all of this."

"All that way to ask Stavros what he thinks?" Petros said. "Ask your mule—it's a shorter walk."

chapter 22

Petros left the basket on the kitchen doorstep. He wanted to avoid Mama, who'd know that Papa had tried to trade the farm. He stopped in the shed and dumped a little feed into the bucket for the chickens. When he came out, he was careful to latch the door again.

He saw Elia heading home. Petros didn't feel good about comparing Stavros to a mule, but he felt worse for the fight with Elia. He wished it hadn't happened, but still, he was glad he'd thought of *something* to say in return.

The chickens came running as Petros swung his arm, casting a handful of feed away from himself. The smaller brown hens were feisty and sometimes got more than their share. He favored the large whites with bare necks.

He heard something scrape the floor of the chicken house and thought a hen must be hurt or sick. Before he could step inside, someone grabbed him crushingly around the face and shoulders. He dropped the feed bucket, fighting hard, trying to scream.

Germans was the first thing to come to mind. He fought harder.

"Yai!" It was a man's voice, a man's strength holding on to him, and then speaking in Greek. "Don't kick and I won't hurt you!"

He pushed Petros into the chicken house, trapping him against the nest boxes. The sharp ends of the hay scratched Petros's face. The earthy smell of the chicken house filled his nose.

Someone else said, "George, George, don't hurt him."

"I haven't hurt him, but he's bruised me many times," George complained, still holding Petros in too firm a grip.

"Boy, boy, stop wriggling," the other one said. "We don't mean you harm. We need a meal. Can you help us?"

Petros stilled, struggling to breathe. The hand covered half his face.

"George, I think you have to let go of him, George."

They set Petros loose. He turned to face two men, both of them dirty, smelly, and wearing clothing cleaner than they were. It struck Petros they'd stolen this shirt from someone's drying laundry. Possibly that was Elia's father's shirt—the large buttons looked the same.

One man was short, the other ugly. George was the ugly one.

"Who are you?" Petros's voice came out like a frog's croak.

"Proud fighters in the Greek army a month ago," the short one said. "Now we are the resistance. We won't surrender."

"I'll bring you something to eat," Petros said, sounding stronger.

"We'll come with you," George said. "The last place we waited they brought a shotgun to send us on our way."

Petros noticed that all of them were breathing fast, like dogs. The men were as frightened as he was. He looked toward the wheat field, hoping to wave to Zola and Old Mario. No luck—they were out of sight.

"From our back step, you can hear everything on the road," Petros said. "If the Germans come, you can hide in the garden."

There was only his sister in the kitchen, stirring a batter. "Sophie—" Petros's warning came too late. She saw strangers and screamed. A rich, blood-chilling scream that stopped Petros short.

"Aieee," the short one cried. "We're hungry. Only hungry."

Mama came running. "I found them in the chicken house," Petros said quickly. "They're resistance."

Mama's face was tight with distrust. But it was Sophie who said, "Every thief is a resister now."

"Shah," Mama said, swatting Sophie. She ordered the men as if they were children. "Sit. I'll feed you. Then you'll go."

"Papa will shoot them," Sophie said, becoming fierce.

"Where's this papa?" George asked Petros.

"Only down the road," Petros said.

The other one grinned. "I think we'll take our chances."

George poked him with an elbow. "Don't be scaring women and children. This is my trouble, that you don't think."

"I thought well enough in the henhouse. You're about to have a meal."

Sophie threw a spatula at them, shouting, "I wish Lambros were here! He would—"

"You know Lambros?" This was George. The other ignored her, only caught the spatula and licked it clean.

"He's our cousin," Petros said. "He climbed the Needle."

"That he did, he did," George said.

"He's our friend," the other one said. "We fought the Germans shoulder to shoulder."

The color had returned to Mama's face. "Eat," she said, setting a loaf of bread on the table. "What are your names?"

"George," they both said.

chapter 23

Mama put cheese on the table, and the Georges began to slice it and eat hungrily. Petros filled glasses with water and sat down with them. "Climbing the Needle," he said. "How was it done?"

The other George said, "Here was our problem. We didn't know the Germans were coming through from the north—"

Sophie set olives and tomatoes in front of them. The Georges stopped talking to put more food in their mouths.

"I thought you were fighting the Italians," Petros said, confused.

"We were—we did," George said. "We fought them into Albania."

Behind them, Mama wet yellow squash flowers in oil and dipped them in a dish of flour. "Then we learned of the Germans at the other border. Our men were needed farther east, around the railways."

"So you let the Italians in," Sophie said, coming back.

"Never say that." Tomato juice dripped down George's chin. "Some may have slipped through, it's true, but the Germans let them in."

The other George said, "We can't argue the difficulties of war with a little girl." This didn't improve Sophie's opinion of them, and she flounced away to help Mama fry the flowers.

George told more of the story. "There were only eighteen of us at the Needle. Each day we won a little, we lost a little. But we stood on Greek soil and plugged the mountain pass."

"We sent rocks down into the gap the Italians were fighting from. Each day they set dynamite and dug. Each day we sent down more rocks. Always they were shooting. Sometimes their bullets made rocks fall," the other George said.

One of them spoke while the other chewed. "It was a standoff. After sixteen days, we were down to seven men."

Mama said, "And the Italians?"

He said, "We didn't count their dead, we counted ours. We were seven and had no food but the oats meant for the mules."

"That's what we ate, chewing grain all day."

"Lambros said we must go down the mountain. Bring back food and volunteers to fight," George said. "He would hold the Italians at bay."

Sophie asked, "What if you were killed?"

Twin shrugs. "At least we would have tried."

She said, "What if Lambros was killed?"

"They weren't killed and neither was Lambros," Petros said when the Georges hesitated. "What happened?"

"We started out on foot," the other George said. "A man on a mule is an easy target. Lambros fired on the Italians all day."

"For six days," George said, "he held them off alone."

The other George took the story back. "In the villages we learned of the surrender. Separately and together, we made our way back to tell Lambros there were new developments."

"We carried food. But we couldn't get to him."

"The Germans came with tanks—tanks. They rolled through the pass with no trouble. The trucks followed. It was the invasion."

"There were no rocks falling. No gunfire." George shook his head. "We figured Lambros for dead."

"While we were saying prayers for him, someone saw a light reflected from the point of the Needle."

"It was there and then it stopped. Some said it was Lambros, some said it was only a trick of the sunlight."

"I held a mirror up and caught sunlight," the other George added. "There was a return signal. We saw the light at the point of the Needle again."

"You understand—Italians were running all over the hillside. German tanks rolling past us," George said. "But three times we signaled and three times we saw light. And then it was gone."

"Everyone agreed Lambros did it. He had nowhere to go but up. He had nothing but fingers and toes for tools to climb that shard."

Petros remembered Lambros didn't look strong enough to climb the Needle. But perhaps that was how a man looked once he'd done it.

George said, "To climb up is one thing, to slide down another. We still counted him a dead man."

"You counted wrong," Sophie said.

chapter 24

When the Georges left, Mama made Petros lock the front gate.

Meanwhile, Old Mario and Zola had come in and heard about the Georges. Everything. Even Petros's part in it, being grabbed in the chicken house, wasn't a fresh story when finally he got a chance to tell it.

Petros went back out to his garden, grumbling to himself about Sophie's big mouth, first turning feet that bled into dying heroes, and now talking as if she had been snatched into the chicken house herself.

Papa brought Stavros home with him. Zola met them at the gate. Petros ran and reached the house as they did, his chest heaving, but by then Zola had told them about the Georges.

Before Petros could protest, Stavros made an excellent point. "How many such men are there? Perhaps the whole Greek army is hiding in villages all over the countryside."

"Many of them," Papa said, and led them inside.

Petros wanted to ask Papa about the deal he'd tried to

strike with the Lemos family, whether Elia had the story straight. But he thought better of it with Stavros sitting there.

"The teachers have moved to the countryside, to houses standing empty," Papa said. "So schools won't open again soon."

"Why would the teachers go?" Sophie asked. "Most are Greek."

"Teachers know the community," Papa said, meaning they knew of anyone who wasn't Greek. Petros understood this much. "They don't want to be questioned."

"Shopkeepers know people," Sophie argued, but her voice was weak with shock.

"Teachers and priests know them best," Zola said, to remind her of things they'd heard on the radio before it was hidden away.

Petros suddenly understood the changes his family had made might not be temporary. If the Germans won the war, this might be the way they were to live the rest of their lives.

"It was my story to tell," Petros complained to Zola when they were alone in their room that night. "I'm the one they grabbed, and I'm the one who brought them into the house—"

"Isn't it enough that it happened to you?"

"It did," Petros agreed. "So I should be the one to tell."

"You think this news should wait until you pull a few more weeds?"

"You saw me come running when Papa came in," Petros said.

"What if I did?" Zola said, waving him away with his hand. "I've lost everything. My books, my puzzles. My maps, my colored pencils. Everything."

"You're just looking for a fight," Petros said.

"I'm looking for my flag." Petros thought his brother had forgotten about the flag in the excitement of writing notes. "Don't give me that fish-eyed look," Zola said. "You threw away my messages. Why not my flag?"

Petros said, "Did you see any flag in the scraps bucket?" He didn't even want to get indignant. This day had used him up.

"It was mine," Petros added. "From the school assembly."

"I kept it for both of us," Zola said.

Now Petros felt a little anger stir in his heart. "If you kept it for both of us, how come I didn't know about it?"

Zola narrowed his eyes, saying, "But you did know about it, didn't you? I hid it from Papa, not from you."

"Why don't you ask Mama?" Petros said, knowing he never would. "Maybe *she* found it."

Zola went to Sophie, who was drying the dishes, and whispered an accusation in her ear. She snapped her dish towel at his legs and gave him such a fight that Mama came in, asking them what it was about.

Zola complained, "Sophie's worse to deal with than her cat."

Petros smiled.

His brother came to stand beside the bed in a bullying way. He hadn't used this manner with Petros in a long time, not since they were both much younger, and Petros found it didn't worry him like it used to. He didn't feel in the least afraid.

Zola even looked a little silly as he stood there another few seconds and then wandered back to his own bed. He looked tired, which they all were, and lost.

Petros was too angry to care. He wanted to tear little bits off the flag and let Zola find them in his bedsheets or in the garden. As bits of blue paper or white, only Zola would know them for something of any importance.

Zola couldn't complain to Papa or Mama without telling them he was guilty of hiding the paper flag. It was a perfect revenge. Zola began to snore.

Petros smothered a laugh. He fell asleep and dreamed he was flying high on the back of a huge blue and white bird.

chapter 25

In the morning, Sophie gave both Petros and Zola several narrow-eyed looks across the breakfast table.

Petros was still angry too and thought his brother looked a little more smug than usual. He wished he could make Zola regret his irritating manner.

Zola busied himself with some chores in the yard, his dog at his heels as he walked around. He hung around the doorway during a short visit from Elia's grandmother and stood at the gate talking to a passerby.

Petros had weeded the rows of basil and nearly-ripe tomatoes before Mama asked Zola why he wasn't working in the garden too.

When Zola finally came to help, Petros was ready to give his brother a hard time.

"This afternoon," Zola said out of the corner of his mouth, as if the tomatoes would repeat his secrets, "Elia's grandmother wants you to go into town with him to get her knitting wool."

Petros's heart leaped, but he said, "It could wait."

"Too late. The trucks," Zola said. He lowered his voice still further. "Haven't you noticed how few are passing the house since yesterday? If the troops are all here, the commander will follow."

Petros nodded. His brother might have a point.

"These are the last notes, and they're ready," Zola said.

Still not wanting to look too willing a partner, Petros said, "Why the last?"

Zola lifted his chin slightly. "Because they are, that's all."

Fifi had climbed out of the goat pen again. She trotted in their direction, stopping to nibble at a reaching tendril of sweet pea. Zola's dog, always careful to avoid Fifi, ambled off to the far end of the row.

"Are you afraid of Papa finding out?"

"I'm afraid of nothing," Zola said. Fifi arrived to bite Zola on the back of his leg. "Ow!" Zola yelled, jumping away from her. "This goat is a menace."

Petros hid a smile and snapped off a nearby stem. "Here, give her a nibble of this sweet pea vine and she won't bite you so hard next time."

"You give it to her," Zola said as Fifi sat down like a good dog would, waiting for a treat. "I won't do her any favors."

Petros fed the goat, saying, "I don't think Elia should help us now that the Germans are here. His family could be safe if he doesn't cause any trouble."

"His family's safe if he isn't caught," Zola said.

"Something could go wrong."

Zola's face darkened. "It's a matter of courage, little brother. We may be frightened, but we fight anyway. That's what a man does."

Petros felt the hair on the back of his neck stand up. Did Zola think he didn't have the courage for this?

chapter 26

Everything went very well at first. Stavros met them in the road and the boys played the game as before, but without laughter or cheers when they made a good catch. Before, it seemed this distracted the eye of anyone watching and it was good. But nerves stole the laughter out of the game.

Petros caught and threw the sand ball and dropped a note whenever he'd found a good place for it, but he saw how different it was this time. At first it was nerves, but when Stavros threw too hard, nerves quickly gave way to anger. They all threw the sand ball to be caught, but threw harder.

Only when the last note was dropped did the boys stop to argue about who threw the sand ball too hard first. The fight ended when Stavros threw the sand ball to the ground hard enough to burst the cloth. Petros expected to share a glance of *there he goes again,* but Elia didn't look at him.

Petros wanted to have something funny to say, or wanted someone else to make a joke, but nothing like that came to any of them. Still, without a word to show he'd been angry or now wasn't, Stavros walked away from the village with them. Petros said, "There won't be any more messages for a time. Zola said so."

"I guessed it," Stavros said. He sounded like this was the worst news he'd gotten since his mother left for the mountains. But also there was a certain relief in his voice.

Elia now felt free to complain that the palms of his hands still hurt. Stavros touched a fresh bruise on his collarbone— Petros thought he had a similar bruise. No one apologized, but all agreed they didn't like catching the sand ball when they'd thrown it so hard.

The boys walked without speaking. Petros thought through the short list of things they'd do when they reached the farm. Everything paled beside the game of sand ball.

"If only we had a kite," Stavros said.

"If only," Elia said. "But with what paper?"

Bumps rose on Petros's arms.

Since the iceman had gone, there was no ice to be had. Mamas wrapped their cheese and meat in newspaper and hung the food in burlap sacks inside the well.

Petros had excellent paper, of course.

"We could steal the paper from the cheese," Stavros said, "if there were cheese." Stavros didn't have a goat. This was the case before the war—Auntie didn't like goats. But her family had always had cheese. Petros felt the shock of this news, but only for a moment.

Whether they seized on this idea—a kite needed a big

piece of paper, the paper needed a frame, the frame needed a tail—or the idea seized them, it made the blood rush, it made them giddy with planning.

"Brown paper. There's still brown paper," Elia said, as if that settled the matter. It didn't, for brown paper was among the many items people had begun to hoard.

Stavros said, "What good is a kite without a tail?"

"Money," Elia said. "It's worthless now." He was right. The tail could be made from some of the useless drachmas Papa kept in boxes under his dresser. It pleased Petros to think of making a kite's tail with the colorful paper money.

"String is hard to find," Stavros said thoughtfully. "If we had a piece of rope . . ."

"That's too heavy for a kite," Petros said. The string had to be thin and light, and yet it must be strong.

"We might unravel the strands," Elia said.

"Not strong enough then," Petros said.

"A thinner rope, then," Stavros said more insistently.

"So even if we have the tail," Elia said, "we don't have string."

Stavros agreed. "A kite must have string. But it needs paper first."

"If we had a genie's lamp, we would have a kite with only one wish," Elia said.

As they turned into the yard, Petros suddenly knew the perfect material for kite string. If only he could get at it. "I think you should stay for dinner," he said to take Stavros's mind off the kite. "We're having beans. If you stay, I won't have to eat my full share."

The boys pulled their slingshots out of their pockets and shot at cans. This was something to do until Mama called out to them, "Don't shoot at my tomatoes."

No one had injured a tomato, but Petros didn't doubt it would happen now that Mama had shouted the likelihood into God's ear. They put their slingshots back in their pockets and settled at the base of the well. They were friends again, and Petros could see that both Elia and Stavros were feeling better for it.

He thought he must be the only one with all they needed, and remained unwilling to tell them so. He hardly understood himself. Never had he kept a secret from Elia, and only rarely would he think of keeping one from Stavros.

He didn't know if he'd keep quiet long or if this secret was going to want telling before the week was out.

chapter 27

That night, when the lights had been turned out all through the house, Zola sat on the edge of his bed so he wouldn't fall asleep. Petros could see the shape of him in the moonlight.

This was the usual way he began a night of writing notes.

Petros pushed up on his elbow and said, "Are you going to be up all night?"

"Shah!"

"We have to stop—"

Zola swooped down on him. "Don't talk about it," he said. He put a hand on Petros's chest that wasn't gentle. "Now go to sleep."

"All right," Petros said.

Zola backed off to sit on the edge of his own bed again. Petros remained lying down, thinking his brother had become a little strange since all this war business had begun. He felt sleep coming to him, sweet and heavy, and he gave himself to it.

In his sleep, he heard Zola talking to himself in that radio voice.

Old Mario and Papa were out at first light to milk the goats. It was the clank of the buckets that got Petros out of bed. That and the delicious smell of boiling coffee. Mama stood at her worktable, chopping onions, tears streaming down her face.

When Mama didn't have time to bake bread, she cooked potatoes in the evening and fried them with onions the next morning. Petros thought it strange at first, but he'd come to like the warm crustiness of potatoes for breakfast.

At the table, Petros was reminded of something he ought to tell. "Stavros and Auntie don't have cheese." Everyone stopped in the act of putting the next bite of potatoes with melted cheese into their mouths. Forks hung in midair.

"Tomorrow," Mama said, "when Sophie and I take cheese and eggs to town to sell, there will be a packet for Auntie. We have more than enough."

With that, all the forks were put into mouths.

Twice it had happened that Mama didn't put hard-boiled eggs on the table to crumble over steamed vegetables. Petros knew when eggs couldn't be served at his family's table, it was because they were placed on someone else's table. He chewed twice as long, knowing cheese might also be rationed.

His family did have more than enough, thanks to a dozen female goats and more chickens. But Petros knew Papa called these ample goats and chickens his insurance policy. Since the day of so many people leaving, Papa had arranged that only half of the eggs and cheese went to market. The rest fed several families who were hungry and who knew Papa's children were Americans.

Petros had never thought of Stavros and Auntie as being among the hungry. He was glad he'd remembered to tell.

From under the table, Zola's dog barked once.

Four men stepped into the kitchen. Two from the back door and two from the front room. They were unshaven, wearing filthy Greek army uniforms. Petros's throat felt too tight to cry out, and yet his last swallow could be tasted there, sharp and sour.

The one closest to him wore unmatched boots, one boot German, one boot Italian. The next one had eyes colored a bright blue. Petros was too frightened to look away.

Not a word was spoken at first, no hand was raised or weapon shown. The manner in which the men moved around them gave the feeling of being surrounded, if only by the few. Papa asked, "What do you want?"

"News of Lambros," one of them said. Shaky with the fright these men had given him, Petros glanced at Zola, who was looking back at him.

"We've heard nothing," Papa said. "Who sent you to us?"

One of the men said, "A friend to you as well as to us."

"What of this?" another of them said, and tossed a crumpled wad of paper onto the table, making everyone but Papa jump. The paper was instantly recognizable to Petros and Zola.

Papa spread the paper out on the table. Zola had gone white.

So had Mama. "My shelf paper," she said, reaching for the note. She smoothed the paper with trembling fingers. She read it in a whisper.

"A boy dropped it." The fellow who threw the paper down was missing two front teeth, but it didn't hamper his speech. The way he leaned in at Papa was scary. "There are more like it."

Mama said, "I thought—I thought I didn't have any more shelf paper. Perhaps someone else had the same kind."

Zola said, "I wrote it," and drew outraged cries from Papa and Mama.

"I knew it was you," Sophie said. She was practically spitting at Zola, like a cat. "Maria *said* this is the kind of thing you would do. I kept saying, no, it couldn't be, and now it *is* you."

Mama turned on Sophie. "Why didn't you tell us?"

"Because I didn't think he'd be so stupid."

Zola bristled at this.

Petros felt as if he ought to say he'd taken part in this. It didn't seem right to let Zola take all the blame.

Papa shouted for quiet.

"I wanted to give people courage," Zola said, looking miserable about it.

Papa said, "When could you accomplish this?"

"While you slept," Zola whispered, "I walked to the village."

chapter 28

Petros couldn't decide which of them this clever lie was meant to protect. Papa was angry, but he'd be much angrier with Zola if he knew the truth. Petros watched Zola, waiting to share knowing this with him, but Zola wouldn't meet his eyes.

Papa said, "You've endangered your sister, your little brother, all of us." Mama echoed these scoldings, although her voice was more sorrowful than angry.

Zola's jaw had firmed in that way he had when he felt unfairly treated. "I only meant to cheer people. I wanted to do something that counts, like Lambros," he said. "I'm too young to join the army. You're too old."

Papa went red in the face.

Old Mario chimed in here, saying, "We're all in the army. Don't we have the fight sitting right here at our table? The boy did what he thought was right. You can't punish him for trying to win a little sooner."

Papa's brows came down like Stavros's.

Old Mario got up and urged the men to eat, pushing the

family's plates at them. He told Mama what to do with this gesture. Feed them.

Mama got up and motioned to the chairs. She pinched Sophie, who hopped up. As hungrily as they glanced at the potatoes and cheese, no one sat until Papa said, "Come."

Sophie began putting the rest of the boiled potatoes and the wedge of cheese in a sack, as if eager to see these fellows on their way. But it might have been only that she needed something more to do, and this was the first thing to come to mind.

The man missing two teeth said, "You didn't know Lambros was captured?"

Papa said, "Where?"

"Athens."

"What was he doing there?"

"In Thebes, Lambros found two British officers in hiding. I knew them," the blue-eyed man said. "They'd been part of the company of men sent here to train our army to fight the Germans. Trapped until Lambros came across them. And starving to death."

Sophie said, "There isn't enough food in Thebes?"

"German soldiers eat first."

"Lambros got them to a safe house in Athens. We were to take over from there, get them to the southern coast. During the night, the Germans came. Wherever food is scarce, there are informers."

The one missing teeth added, "Lambros slept at the open

window and heard too many cars coming. He led us all out of the house and over the rooftops. He walks a narrow board like a goat, crossing the city from roof to roof. That night we were all goats, knowing the Germans were coming in below."

"How did *you* do it?" Sophie asked.

"Lambros held one end of a rope, we held the other. He was pulling, we stepped quickly. The rope allowed us to feel we were safe, and before we could take a wrong step, we were on the other side."

"The man outsmarted our fear," one of them said.

"That night Lambros saved us," another said. "He saved the officers, and the fellow who owned the house and me. Four lives that would be over now."

"What happened this time?" Papa asked. "When he was captured."

"No doubt someone told the Gestapo where to find him," the blue-eyed man said. "We hoped he escaped."

"No one escapes," another said with his mouth full. He went back to devouring potatoes and cheese.

The blue-eyed man looked angry. "Someone saw him walk out of there. He's been lucky before."

"If he's lucky," the man missing teeth said, "he's dead."

Sophie dropped a glass and began to cry as it shattered. Petros's heart stopped, then beat too fast. Mama put her arms around Sophie, but also told her to get the broom.

Papa said, "Go to the gate, Petros. Keep watch."

Petros ran to see if the road was clear of trucks and

Omeroses. He went back to stand beneath the window, where he could see the gate and still hope to hear what was being said.

Mama asked a question, and although he didn't hear her clearly, he heard the answer. "Lambros led the highest-ranking British officer to Athens, where he hoped to put him in the hands of those who are smuggling the remaining British soldiers out of the country."

"But how can you know Lambros was captured?" Sophie cried.

"There are many spies," one of the men said. "Collaborators. It's difficult to move through Athens and avoid them."

"Does his family know?" Papa asked.

"We can't go to his family," another of them said. "Lambros has embarrassed the Germans too many times. They'll be watched."

"I'll tell them," Papa said.

"You must be careful too," one of the men said. "If they learn you're his uncle, they may want to question you." Petros ran and climbed the mulberry tree in case Papa went to Auntie immediately.

Then again, maybe he wouldn't go at all. Papa didn't want the Germans to notice him or his family. It was everything Papa tried to do, look like an ordinary Greek.

It came as a shock to realize the danger Lambros carried with him was like an illness, catching. Petros almost hoped Papa wouldn't go. And yet, how could they do nothing to tell Lambros's family what had happened to him?

After a few minutes, he got a little nervous, thinking he'd come to the tree too quickly—he might have missed something of interest. The longer Papa didn't come, the more he was tempted to climb down and go back to the window.

But he didn't care to be caught listening in when he was supposed to be watching the road. He fidgeted with indecision until he saw a movement in the garden, at some distance from the house. He had no doubt the four men were leaving.

For the first time he considered the luck of it. They were alone in the house when these men arrived, no German commander to be considered. Or maybe it wasn't so much luck as a matter of the men watching them for a time to be sure.

And then he considered the meaning of Lambros's being captured. Elia's grandfather had once said "captured by the Gestapo" meant the same thing as "soon dead," and no one disputed it.

He couldn't think of Lambros as soon dead. His heart fought it and his mind wouldn't listen. Was this what Papa was going to tell Stavros and Auntie? The idea sickened him.

Papa came out the front door at that moment, walking like a man with unpleasant business. Zola, a step behind him, carried what Petros guessed to be a packet of cheese. The dog followed Zola as far as the gate, his tail held at a dejected angle.

Petros thought Zola must've asked to go. Perhaps Papa wasn't so angry with him after all. "Warn your mother if anyone comes," Papa said as he passed under the tree.

chapter 29

Mama called him inside a few minutes later. She took Petros and Sophie up to the flat roof of the house. They swept it clean of dried leaves and bits of twig and an old bird nest built in the twist of iron table legs.

Before the air raids at Easter, the family often ate dinner up on the roof at a large round table. They slept there in summer, when the house was too hot for an easy sleep. From here Mama could see the countryside for miles in any direction—she could see Papa and Zola.

"Do you remember when Zola made his parachute?" Petros asked Mama, and pointed at the nearly chest-high barrier at the edge of the roof, the breakfall. He could see over it with ease now, but until he was five, Papa'd held him up to look. "He threw the cat down just there."

Mama slapped her face with the memory of it. "The devil," she said, almost fondly. It was often this way, Mama cherishing the memories of things she had punished them for. Petros wondered why she couldn't appreciate these adventures more at the time they happened.

"It was a fine parachute," Petros said.

"Who would have expected such a contraption to work?" Mama said, laughing.

Sophie said, "Don't talk like *I've* forgiven him. My cat spooks if I flap a sheet over my bed. She mistakes it for the tablecloth."

"Your cat hasn't forgotten Zola either," Petros said. The cat often hid under the bed so she could leap out and bite Zola around the ankles. She troubled no one else this way.

Mama made an annoyed sound with her tongue.

Once they'd finished on the roof, Mama urged them to scrub the parlor floor and polish the remaining pieces of wood furniture.

Petros grumbled a little, and she said, "You're lucky there's no silver to polish, or linen to press."

Petros didn't feel lucky, but he eyed the blue draperies, thinking thoughts of silken blue kite string.

Papa and Zola were gone for two hours, at the least. They came through the gate, and Zola peeled off to walk in the orchard.

Petros caught up with him under the peach trees. "Well?"

Zola said, "Auntie told us Aunt Hypatia is sometimes here, sometimes in the mountains."

"Stavros never said anything," Petros said.

"That's what he should say," Zola said. "Nothing."

He was in the mood for a fight, but Petros didn't give it to him. "What about the notes?"

"Auntie forgives me."

"Forgives you?"

"Papa blames me," Zola complained. "Papa's old, and afraid someone might tell them about us. He doesn't care about victory. He wants to be safe."

Petros kept silent. Much of the time he felt exactly that way. He wanted life to go back to the way it had been before the Germans invaded, even before the Greeks were at war with the Italians. It was good.

And now things were changed. No one knew yet what it would mean.

"It's not fair," Zola said. "Lambros was captured before I had written anything about him."

"Where did those four men go?" Petros asked.

"Papa told them how to find old Mr. Katzen's house," Zola said. "No one goes up there now. It's too far from the village. The weeds hide it."

"Why is that?"

"He's gone," Zola said. "The Germans came and he was gone."

Petros sometimes thought of Mr. Katzen as he tended his peppers. But there were many things to think about once he'd left the peppers behind, and he'd forgotten to wonder why he hadn't seen the old man lately. He cringed from knowing this, but there it was.

chapter 30

Working in his garden that afternoon, Petros began to protect
that pepper plant, putting a bit of gauze over it to keep the
bugs off. When the fruit was ready, he'd save the seeds for
next year. He'd remember Mr. Katzen.

During the afternoon rest, when even Zola slept—since
missing so much sleep, he seemed to appreciate it more—
Petros went to the arbor and cut a long vine. He stripped it of
leaves and tiny green grapes. He broke the stem to shape a
hexagon. The shape of his kite.

He wished, momentarily, that he'd told Zola. It seemed
selfish to keep something so fine to himself. Perhaps he
should have told Stavros and Elia too, but it wasn't their feelings that weighed on him.

The division of big brother/little brother always made
Petros unhappy. Perhaps it even made Zola unhappy. Now
and again Petros wanted to do things differently.

He struggled with many such discomforts lately, from
wanting to do things so he felt right about them and then *having* to do them in a way that felt wrong. The kite was one of

these things. If he thought the matter through, he might find a compromise. He could do that later. He would.

But this hour couldn't be wasted.

Working carefully, he strengthened the corners of the kite with thinner tendrils of the vine. He climbed the arbor, set the frame on top of the thick ceiling of grape vines, and left it to dry stiff and strong in the sun.

Petros carried the wilted branches and scraps of grape leaves to the goats. All the evidence of his labor was gone in minutes. He let Fifi out of the pen, still thinking of how to get the string he had in mind.

The next morning, Papa made his marketing trip to the village. Mama and Sophie were already waiting in the truck, having packed cheese and eggs for Auntie.

Petros waited only until the truck was out of sight before leaving his garden. A better time for the tedious work of gluing the paper to the frame could not have been arranged.

Old Mario and Zola were on the far side of the garden. They believed Petros to be working in his. He retrieved the paper flag, being careful not to squeeze creases into it, and carried the frame in his other hand.

Sophie's cat lay curled on the doorstep, a sleeping guardian. Everything was as he'd hoped. The quiet of the house was almost like being in a cave.

Petros took all his materials to his room to work on the kite. The paste wouldn't pick up dust and leafy debris as it would if he worked in the shelter of the arbor, and he could hide the finished kite under his bed until it dried.

There was no one to scold when he spilled a little flour on the floor. He wiped it up before going on to the next step, adding the water a little at a time, stirring the paste with a knife.

Petros loved the rattle of paper, the stickiness of paste. He loved the kite, now becoming more than a dream he watched in his mind's eye. The paper still wanted to curl as he flattened it, but this made it easier to glue to the grapevine frame. The scissors, only last year just a little too big for his hands, worked smoothly, without fraying the edges where he cut. It was as if he were singing a song of kite making, and all the notes were perfect.

He wiped his sticky fingers on his shirt again and again as he folded the edges of the paper flag to the frame. The strong blue and white could be seen on the backs of his eyelids when he blinked. Every minute flew by so fast, he didn't know how much time had passed.

The thought came to him to show Zola the kite before it was quite finished. His brother might be angry for a moment, for an hour even, but then the kite would win him over. He imagined he and Zola would work on it together, tying up each corner of the frame with the blue silk, light enough for the kite to carry it, strong enough to hold the kite captive, and of a color that would fade from the eye so the kite would seem to fly as freely as a bird.

The kite would take a while to dry—this was a worry. Petros was so intent on making this kite of all kites that he heard nothing until he heard Zola's breath, drawn in fast. "I knew it," Zola said in a voice held low and—this pleased Petros—excited. Not angry.

"I didn't mean—" to keep it from Zola, not really. He meant to protect it. From Mama, Sophie, all of them. That's what he wanted to say.

But Zola interrupted him. "Shah. Hide it. Papa's coming in."

"They're back?" Petros hadn't heard the truck.

"Just Papa. Mama and Sophie are sitting with Auntie for a while."

He helped Petros slide the kite carefully under his bed. It was still wet in places but already sturdy as it disappeared into the shadows.

Papa and Old Mario entered the kitchen, disagreeing about something. Zola said, "Change your shirt. Clean up this mess." And then he hurried out of the room so fast his shirt-tail fluttered.

After a panicky look around, Petros shoved the cup of paste under Zola's bed. Paper scraps and the scissors went under the rug. He yanked off his shirt and wiped up the bits of paste drying on the floor.

Wearing a clean shirt, he looked into the small mirror on the dresser to be sure he didn't have paste in his hair. He put an innocent look on his face.

In the kitchen, there was talk of buying a donkey and cart.

Papa was slicing tomatoes that were still warm from the sun, Old Mario sprinkling oil and oregano on chunks of dried bread.

Zola had taken a view that didn't agree with Papa or Old Mario, a useful distraction. His dog had curled under the table like a dollop of soft cheese. No one took particular notice of Petros as he joined them.

While they ate, whenever he looked at his brother, Zola wore an expression of deep thought. Petros knew his brother was thinking of the kite. Petros thought he was angry after all.

But when they went to their room later, Zola's eyes flashed with something like joy. "It's a fine effort," he said admiringly.

"It's mine."

"It's ours."

Petros thought this over. Wasn't this exactly what he'd hoped they might do? Share the kite? But the work was his. And the work wasn't done. "It's not ready to fly."

"No," Zola agreed. "But someday we'll fly it."

Petros said, "When I get the string, we'll fly it."

"Where will you find string?"

"I won't tell you," Petros said. "The kite is—the making of it is mine."

"Very well," Zola said. "But the hiding of it is something we must do together. We can't leave it under the bed. The roof!"

Petros shook his head. "Papa might go up there."

"I didn't say we'll leave it in plain sight," Zola said, a little of the sneering big brother creeping into his voice. "We'll put it on the roof of the stairwell."

"A plane could see it," Petros said, happy to spot the flaw in Zola's planning. "Or it might blow away. It's a kite, after all."

Zola looked stymied for a minute. Then he said, "The back wall of the stairwell is inches from the breakfall. The space is little more than a crevice."

"True," Petros said. "The trellis covers that wall. No one will look there." The trellis started at the ground but had been built up to cover the structure of the stairwell with vines.

"We'll put it between the wall and the breakfall, hidden by the trellis."

This was a good plan. Petros might not have thought of it himself, although he didn't say so. Instead, he said, "Even the commander couldn't find it there."

chapter 31

While the afternoon sun baked the soil, Petros worked in his garden. He wanted to make up the time lost working on the kite.

When it was about time the others would be waking up, he washed his hands in a small bucket beside the well. Fifi butted against him, hoping for an extra treat—a bit of carrot or a leaf from a pepper plant. "You were lucky today," Petros said, holding a frothy green fringe of sweet fennel in front of her nose. "I broke this small branch."

Fifi snatched it from him and chewed.

"Hssst! Petros!"

Petros heard this whisper like it came out of the air over his head, and he looked up.

"It's me, Lambros."

This time the whisper could be felt like a breath on his neck.

"Are you a ghost?"

When Lambros laughed, the sound echoed out of the well. "Not yet, small cousin. Not yet."

But when Petros leaned over the well to look inside, and saw Lambros lying in one of the water buckets, he still wouldn't have known him.

Lambros's face was bruised and cut over the eyebrow and on the cheekbone. He held his left hand to his chest, and one finger stuck out at an odd angle. Petros's stomach turned over.

"I'll get Papa," he said.

"Wait," Lambros said. "He'll come soon enough. Tell me who else is around. Any Germans?"

"Not yet," Petros said. "Perhaps tomorrow. There were other men here yesterday, looking for you."

"Gestapo?"

"No, no. Like you."

Lambros nodded. Petros thought the news heartened him.

"Old Mario's coming," Petros said, seeing him out of the corner of his eye.

"Don't let him turn on the well or I'll drown for sure."

Petros went straight to Old Mario and said everything right into his hairy left ear, which was the one that heard best.

"Bless him," Old Mario said. He hurried over to the well, looked down, and said, "Bless you, boy. No one has escaped them but you."

"Let us hope I continue to be so blessed," Lambros said. "And you along with me. I hope it's all right I came here."

Petros and Old Mario looked up to see Papa coming toward them, carrying a small bucket of tomatoes, and probably asking himself why they were looking into the well.

"Is there trouble?" he called to them.

Petros signaled with his head, no, then realized it was indeed trouble. It was only not the trouble Papa meant.

When Papa reached them and looked down the well, he didn't speak right away. When finally he did, he said, "I'm glad you aren't killed."

Lambros laughed a little. "Some of this damage I did to myself. I caught a ride on the fender of a truck, but when it hit a bump, I was thrown off."

"We'll get you out of there," Papa said.

"Uncle, I'm sorry," Lambros said. "When my grandfather built his house and set up his loom on such a busy thoroughfare, he didn't anticipate how hard it would be to get through the village when it's overrun with an occupying army."

"He knew you could come here," Papa said.

Old Mario said, "Lemos likes a cup of coffee after his nap, but the family may be in the garden by now."

Papa yanked on a rope and pulled up a sack from inside the well. He said, "The season's first artichokes. Petros, take them to the Lemos kitchen. If the family's all there, stay ten minutes, visiting. If not, hurry back so we'll know to wait till dark."

Lambros's cuts were tended to most easily, washed with vinegar and a stitch taken by the time Petros returned. Papa decided the finger wasn't exactly broken. He yanked on it to make it take its proper place in the joint. It was over quickly and Lambros didn't make a sound. It was hunger and exhaustion that took the greatest toll on him.

"We heard you were captured," Papa said when he'd finished being the doctor.

"They left me alone in a room," Lambros said. "It was deep inside the building, no windows."

Old Mario set a bowl of lentil soup in front of Lambros. He asked, "How did you get away?"

"The Germans grow overconfident. Once I was alone, I counted to five and opened the door. A washerwoman was there, mopping the floor. She said nothing but pointed to a hallway, then made a motion with her hands. Right, left, right."

Papa and Old Mario grinned..

"I went down the hall, then right, left, right," Lambros said. "Out the door and into a crowd of fellow Greeks, informers all. They thought me to be one of them and nodded as I passed by. I turned a corner and made myself look like someone with a place to go. Then I came home."

"Where else would you go?" Old Mario asked him when Lambros couldn't say more.

"I see we've been invaded since I was here last," Lambros said in a near whisper. "I've put you in grave danger, Uncle."

"Not if we hide you well enough," Papa said.

"The roof?" Old Mario asked.

"For tonight, perhaps. We'll put you back in the well for now," Papa said. "The third tunnel as you climb down, it's mostly dry."

"Thank you, Uncle."

Papa shook his head. He didn't like to be thanked.

"You must get a message to Uncle Spiro," Lambros said. "He'll know if there's someone I might travel with. Another soldier."

Papa said, "Spiro?"

"Yes, Uncle. If I could have made it the rest of the way, I wouldn't trouble you."

"Petros, make up a sack for your uncle," Papa said. "Something he likes and may have in short supply. A jar of honey. Coffee. Bread. Tell your uncle Spiro of our visitor."

"Yes, Papa." Petros was careful not to sound too pleased.

chapter 32

Petros thought of a dozen things he wanted to tell Uncle Spiro, on his way to the other farm. He could hardly keep his mind on one bit of news before his thoughts turned as if blown on the wind he imagined for the kite.

He would tell Uncle Spiro Lambros was safe, of course. He'd say there were two valuables in the well. The glass marble. Uncle Spiro should know what a fine shooter it was.

And Lambros.

His spirits were excellent up to that point. After all, most of what he had to tell was good news. Only the end of the war felt uncertain, something to be waited for with a kind of dread, like the German commander.

But he'd also tell about the Georges, an interesting story Uncle Spiro would know nothing about. He told it to himself a couple of times as he trudged along. He'd come to the border of the farm when Uncle Spiro called his name.

Uncle Spiro sat at the top of a knoll, and Lump stood beside him, munching grass. When the little goat saw Petros, he came bucketing down the hill like a rocking horse. He butted Petros playfully.

"You teach your goats bad manners, Uncle Spiro," he said, laughing. He climbed the hill to sit beside his uncle. "I've come with news."

Uncle Spiro offered a crust pulled out of his roomy pants pocket. "You look pale, boy. Are you hungry?"

"A little. I brought honey."

Uncle Spiro looked into Petros's sack. "It's very poor bread we buy now. I could bake it for myself, but wheat is scarce— no one will trade it." He shook his head as if the situation dizzied him.

"Perhaps you could talk to Papa," Petros said, a little smile in his heart. "He grows wheat."

"You're a sly boy," Uncle Spiro said, opening the jar of honey.

Patient until now, Petros's stomach growled as loudly as an animal wanting to be fed. They shared the bread, dipping it into the honey.

It took only a minute to tell Uncle Spiro everything of great importance. "He said—I think he said you would know of any soldiers he could travel with." Only now did Petros question why Lambros thought Uncle Spiro would be the one to know.

"Those four who came to your house," Uncle Spiro said. "In what direction did they travel?"

Petros told him about Mr. Katzen, that the house stood

empty so far as anyone knew. But also there was no certainty these men stopped there.

"No, but it's a place to start looking," Uncle Spiro said. "Tell your papa he'll have to manage for a couple of days."

Petros nodded. "Then what?"

"Nothing is certain."

When Petros returned home, Lambros had been hidden in the well. This he knew because everyone had returned to work. Except Papa, who was staying close to the house.

He stopped chasing Fifi long enough to complain that she'd broken into the shed and filled her belly with chicken feed. That much grain could kill a goat. "Get her up every time you see her lie down," he told Petros. "Don't let her rest until she's digested that feed."

Old Mario had driven into the village and returned with Mama and Sophie. They weeded around the bushy mounds of bitter dandelion. Mama called out requests for odd jobs and little repairs, glad to have Papa so nearby.

Otherwise, the ordinary work of late in the day had begun.

Old Mario started the well. The belt whined overhead, the buckets rose and fell, the water spilled. In the heat of the day, the squash leaves drooped as if the plants were dying, but in the cool of the evening, every evening, they recovered.

They sat down to an early meal of spaghetti with fried greens and olives. Mama and Sophie and Old Mario had come home with news of the village, but all of it had the ring of complaints, not of news.

"Isn't it strange that we don't hear any talk of the war?" Zola asked.

"No one's talking about anything but the weather and their bunions," Papa said. "They wait."

"Don't rush bad news," Old Mario said from his end of the table, and Papa agreed. As if Old Mario's words were a prediction, they heard the growl of trucks coming down the road and the squeal of brakes at the gate.

For a moment no one moved. Sophie began to cry.

"Shah!" Mama said.

Two trucks and a jeep carrying officers came to a halt in front of the house, the motors running.

"Don't turn off the well," Papa said. Petros wondered if Lambros could hear the trucks or if the clank of the buckets covered the noise.

Half a dozen German soldiers, boys of about Zola's age from the look of them, followed a leader up to the veranda. They looked as weary as Old Mario had looked after losing the night's sleep in burying their belongings.

There were no apologies as they carried Mama's furniture out to the trucks, but it was done quickly. Petros stood with his family in the yard, feeling oddly embarrassed. He could see Zola's frustration at their helplessness, could see the determination with which Papa met that same helplessness.

Just as the ordeal should have been over, the leader went

into the house. He opened the door as if the house were his, and he let the others in. Mama and Papa—in fact everyone—followed him inside.

He pointed at the china cabinet and the chandelier.

"No," Mama said, and Papa put a hand on her arm, reminding her. A soldier who'd come to the doorway signaled to the others, and in a moment the parlor was invaded.

The leader sent Petros outside with a wave of his hand. Papa nodded. Petros stopped beneath one of the persimmon trees flanking the gate. From there he could see everything that happened at his house and at the Lemoses' house.

The air stank with the fumes from the growling motors.

The china cabinet, emptied of the pottery Mama had placed there to disguise the lack of dishes and crystal, was carried away in two pieces. Petros had never thought of it as something that might be moved.

The soldiers weren't dressed for this work. Their uniforms stretched over their backs so tightly Petros heard stitches pop more than once. Sweat streamed down the soldiers' faces, and wet patches began to appear on their jackets.

Mama scolded the two soldiers who first attempted to roll the chandelier over the edge of the veranda. Despite the leader, who moved to stop her, Mama didn't hesitate to grab another young soldier by the arm and enlist his labor.

In very short order, two men were carrying the chandelier overhead like Cleopatra's couch. His mother followed them out to the truck with an odd mixture of pride and heartsickness

148

etched on her face. Out in the road, Grandmother Lemos ran to meet Mama with outstretched arms.

Her furniture was being loaded onto a truck too. Elia stood near his mother. An officer coming from the Lemoses' house crossed the street to oversee the men. When this one's gaze touched Petros, he felt a chill, like leaning over the well.

It felt as if the man didn't see Petros and his family as people but as male goats, not useful for very long. The officer didn't go into the house but pointed to the shades on the veranda. He spoke sharply to Papa, who didn't appear to understand.

Petros saw it all happen.

chapter 33

The officer climbed the steps, repeating what he'd said. When Papa didn't move, the officer raised a hand. Zola quickly stepped forward to reach for the roller shades the officer had pointed at. Their father moved then too, to help Zola take the shades down.

When the shades had been put into the arms of one of the sweating soldiers, the officer focused on Zola. It was the same question over and over that Zola didn't answer, and the officer's voice rising.

Petros stood on one foot, then the other, wanting to help. But what should he do, what would Papa want him to do?

Mama grabbed Petros around the shoulders and held on to him so tightly he could hardly breathe. "Don't move from here," she said. "Let your papa take care of this."

The officer finally screamed the same words in frustration. He slapped Zola with the back of his hand.

Petros flinched.

Sophie shrieked, then fell silent.

Zola had cringed away from the officer and begun to cry. He said something in Greek—words so garbled by furious tears, Petros could understand nothing. He couldn't think of a time when he'd known Zola to cry.

Petros was dimly aware of the sound of guns being shaken into position to defend the officer. Of the Lemos family calling to each other. Papa put his arms around Zola the way Mama still held Petros, Papa looking both humble and outraged.

Old Mario came around the house with a pitchfork in his hand. Immediately a soldier pointed a rifle at him, forcing him to put the pitchfork on the ground.

Papa stood with his shoulders hunched in a manner Petros didn't recognize. He spoke continuously in a low, calming voice, always looking at the soldier.

Zola pointed, over and over, to the place where the shades had been, saying he'd given the officer what he'd pointed at. Zola spoke only Greek.

Another officer and a translator came through the yard, the translator shouting in Greek that no one was to move. There were explanations on the veranda, but no apologies.

The officer shouted things at his men. A soldier shouted at Papa, something Petros didn't understand. But he saw the way his father straightened up, pushing Zola into the house and out of sight.

The soldiers marched back across the yard and out through the gate, heavy boots making the ground tremble. The metal they wore clashed in Petros's ears as they passed by. He got the strong idea he'd be full of bruises if they only brushed against him.

It took a few minutes more for the last of the household goods to be packed on the trucks, and for the soldiers to board. They took the pitchfork and the pointed hoes with them. Except that Grandmother Lemos kept on crying, both families watched in a kind of stunned silence.

The trucks left with an even greater noise. The fumes hung in the air like a cloud. Petros ran for the house.

Papa came out, hurrying to Mama. But Grandmother Lemos got to her first. The women hugged as if they hadn't seen each other in weeks. Grandfather Lemos grabbed Papa around the shoulders in the same way.

Petros crossed the veranda and stepped into the strangely naked-looking parlor. Zola looked pink around the eyes but otherwise the same. Smaller, but then, the parlor looked so much larger.

"You thought fast, looking so angry and afraid at the same time," Petros said. "I don't know that I could pretend so well."

Zola's face reddened. "I wasn't pretending."

"That's what I mean, then," Petros said. "You did exactly right."

Elia's mother and father stood across the road for perhaps a full minute, Elia and his sister beside them, before they joined the rest in Mama's parlor. Everyone spoke at the same time, and questions went unanswered; no one seemed quite capable of really talking to each other.

The boys followed this confusion from room to room, as if they were much younger and weren't sure how to behave, even Zola. The dog came in from the hallway, and Zola bent to scratch his ears. No one asked where the dog had gone when the Germans came. The last thing they needed was a dog brave enough to get shot in front of their eyes. The dog only needed to face stray cats trying to get into the chicken house.

"We've been to more cheerful funerals," Zola whispered to Petros.

The families walked through each other's houses, now emptied of treasures and looking hardly like the places they'd lived in that morning. Soon they were joined by the Omeros family from down the road.

"We're to guard the phone lines for three miles," Mr. Omeros said. "My boys and me. Guard them from our own army."

This news had been on the radio, Greek citizens made to do the German army's job, keep the phone lines safe, keep roads clear, and if they failed, they were killed.

Papa told them Mama was expected to cook and clean for the commander, and Zola added that he'd be arriving one day soon. Even Papa looked surprised.

"How do you know this?" Mr. Omeros asked.

Out of habit now, their family spoke only Greek. Zola hesitated, then said, "I heard them say so."

Mr. Omeros nodded. In this way the neighbors ignored

Zola's mistake. But also, Petros saw that Mr. Omeros considered this to be worse news than his own.

Sophie said, "The commander will be much like this one, an animal."

Grandmother Lemos suggested poisoning him slowly, and for an instant Petros saw on his mother's face she wished it was something to be considered. "No," she said. "The minute he falls ill, we'll be expected to take the first bite. After him, there would come another."

Mrs. Omeros began to cry. The women gathered around her and moved to a bedroom to talk. Old Mario walked outside and turned off the well, giving the boys their first opportunity to escape the adults. Going to the veranda, Papa lit his cigarette, and the other men sat down with him.

Settling themselves under the arbor, Petros, Elia, and Zola brought out their slingshots and tried to put holes in the leaves, a trick of shooting the tiniest stones very hard.

Once in a while a small bunch of unripened grapes hit the ground. "Those were yours," the shooter would say to the others. The boys buried them hastily, before Papa could complain of the grapes he wouldn't get to harvest in midsummer.

chapter 34

The air began to be sweet with odors of Grandfather Lemos's pipe tobacco and frying onions. In the back of Petros's mind, always, there was knowing Lambros was cold and probably hungry, but there was no way to hurry anyone home.

When now and again Papa's eyes met and held Petros's glance, he knew that Lambros was in the back of Papa's mind too. Lambros was safe—that was the important thing to be glad for. They were all safe. When the Omeroses left, all of Elia's family crossed the road to go home. Going off with Zola to milk the goats, Petros asked, "Do you think Lambros could hear the trucks?"

"Either that or he thought we had an earthquake," Zola said.

Old Mario joined them at the goat pen to help with the milking. "When people are upset, sometimes they stare out of windows," he said quietly. "We must do the things they expect to see."

Petros thought that meant they all had to go back to work until nightfall. It wasn't that far off. Already the sun was low in the sky.

But Papa came over as they finished with the goats and said, "Go inside, Petros, and ask Mama for a dark blanket and to boil some coffee."

Petros found Mama in the kitchen. She and Sophie were heating water so they could wrap Lambros with hot wet towels. "Take those rolled blankets up to the roof," Mama told Petros.

"Lambros will sleep on the roof?"

"Old Mario will sleep on the roof," Mama said. "Lambros will have a bed until sunup."

"Papa wants one of these blankets for Lambros now."

Zola had gone out to the roadside and was hacking at weeds with a rusted scythe found at the back of the garden. Papa had already helped Lambros into a wheelbarrow and covered him with the blanket. Petros walked alongside them with an armful of rakes as Papa pushed Lambros to the kitchen door.

Once inside, Papa and Old Mario tended him. There was a constant exchange of hot and cooled towels at first, and no shortage of stories to tell.

Petros asked, "What was it like to climb the Needle, Lambros?"

"Hard work, little cousin, at first. But also clean. The wind was strong, the air fresh, my muscles glad." Lambros chewed through another bite of hot fried potato. He could devour anything set before him.

He went on, saying, "The hardest part came at the end,

where the top is chopped up like stair steps. My feet were wet with blood and sweat. It was all I could do not to slip off. Also to remember I'm not an angel."

Everyone in the kitchen stood fearfully quiet.

"An angel?" This was Mama.

"It was the shirt billowing at my back," Lambros said. "After hours of climbing, in my fevered mind I thought I had wings. I imagined I could fly."

"What did you do?" Sophie asked him.

"I reached the top," Lambros said. "I lay on my back to let my heart get on with the business of beating. I heard the swoosh of blood in my veins. Looked at the blue curve of the sky where it met darkness. Felt the earth turning as if the Needle runs through the center like an axle. I floated like a dandelion seed. It's a climb I must do again one day."

"You have to do it with ropes," Papa said.

Lambros shook his head. "It will never be the same."

"No," Sophie said, almost sadly. "But at least we'll know you'll live through it."

Lambros laughed. "You're going to be a practical woman, cousin."

When Zola came in, Mama and Sophie set dinner out on the table. The family kept Lambros company in the shadows of the kitchen until a late hour, the only light coming from the stove.

* * *

No one got a good night's sleep.

When Mama finally sent Sophie and the boys to bed, Zola sat up in the darkness of the bedroom.

"What are you up to?" Petros whispered.

"Nothing," Zola said. "Go to sleep."

Petros sat up.

"You must go to sleep," Zola said. "Papa wants to bring the radio upstairs again."

"Again?" Little bumps came out on Petros's arms.

"He brought it upstairs in the middle of the night once and listened in the dark," Zola said. "I know because I helped him move my bed. You slept through it all. Mama too."

"I don't believe you," Petros said. Zola didn't argue.

Petros lay down to think the matter over, recalling he'd thought he dreamed this one night, and he began to believe Zola. After a few minutes, he pretended to be asleep.

When Papa came in to move the bed, Zola helped. They went to the kitchen together, and then Petros heard the low but definite voice of someone on the radio. There was also a little clatter of bread pans. Petros sat near the door, trying to hear.

A few minutes later he heard Mama hurry along the hall in bare feet, and then she scolded Papa in whispers. When she didn't come back and the radio voice went on, Petros crept out into the hall. Soon all but Petros and Sophie sat in the kitchen, listening to the radio station from Cairo.

An hour later Lambros went out to sleep in Old Mario's

bed and Petros hurried back to his own, to pretend he was sleeping again. He dreamed all night of fighting planes and German soldiers built of rock.

They were all up again before daybreak. Papa and Old Mario sat quietly, drinking hot coffee with Lambros. Mama dropped a whole loaf of the bread into a sack, to be eaten with cheese and tomatoes belowground.

"A knife," Sophie said, trying to think of everything.

"I have a knife," Lambros said quietly.

"Grandfather's jacket," Petros said, and Old Mario made an approving sound in his throat.

The jacket hung by the door. Grandfather had died four years ago, but his sheep's-wool jacket passed from hand to hand around the house as needed, to be used as baby blanket, knee warmer, shawl. He would like that it kept Lambros warm. Zola lifted the jacket off the hook.

When everyone would have gone outside, Papa halted them. "Old Mario will take you out there," Papa said. "We shouldn't have a parade at this hour." He stood in the doorway, Petros and Zola at his side.

When Lambros had climbed down, Papa said, "We must think of how to keep him in the sunshine. But we must also think of how we might be safe at the same time."

"The roof," Petros said, the first thought to pop into his head.

"To be trapped up there if the trucks come again?" Papa said. "He must be able to get to the well from wherever he is."

"I'll think, Papa," Zola said.

"We'll think of a plan," Petros agreed.

Zola looked as if he were about to remark on this, but Papa gave them both a hard look. No fighting, the look said.

Because Lambros was in the well, Mama told Petros and Zola to go no farther away from the house than the garden. Even the mulberry tree was out of the question—Papa kept the gate locked.

chapter 35

Instead of eating at midday, Old Mario took his old bones to his bed. Zola slept through the high heat of the afternoon, the dog lay on the cool marble floor. Papa snored in the bedroom at the other end of the house.

Mired in the first quiet hour of the high heat, Petros spent several minutes thinking, but not about Lambros. Then he tiptoed into the parlor.

Only slivers of the afternoon light seeped into the room between gaps in the blue velvet drapes.

Easy chairs sat in the gloom like thoughtful elephants, floor lamps stood on one leg like strange birds. Where the chandelier used to hang, only a memory remained.

Behind him, somewhere in the house, Petros heard a sound like the scuff of a sandal on the floor. Possibly Sophie. Petros scurried across the room and slipped into the space behind the drapes. He had enough room to stand without touching them.

He listened, holding his breath.

The parlor windows started close to the floor and rose

nearly to the ceiling, so that he felt the sill at the back of his leg, above his ankles, and the bottom of the open window at the back of his head.

He listened for footsteps in the hallway, but could hear nothing more. When he relaxed, he made a discovery. Even though the shutters were closed behind him, the light was brighter here than inside the room. Bright enough to work by.

Petros sat so he fitted into the space between the window and the folds of the soft fabric, and he was hidden from anyone who might pass by on their way to the kitchen. Because the shutters were closed against the light, he couldn't be seen from the outside.

He had perhaps an hour to do his work, maybe a little more.

At the bottom of the drapes hung a thick silk fringe, twelve inches long at least. It was this fringe that interested him. Petros separated one thin silk cord from the many, gave it a hard tug, and was thrilled to feel it pull free quite easily. A small miracle.

He traced the strand to its other end with his fingertips and tugged again. Now he had about two feet of thin silk cord to call his own. Carefully, he singled out another strand.

When Petros had four strands of cord, he inspected the fringe. It didn't look especially thinner. He couldn't even find the exact places he'd taken the pieces from. His mother would never notice the missing strands either.

This was exactly as he had hoped but doubted it would be.

Still, it would take many such afternoons to get enough strands of the fringe knotted together and balled up. Thinking this, Petros looked at the place where the fringe joined the velvet.

A deep row of several narrow braids of the same silk covered the stitching at the top of the fringe. Petros suspected he'd get much longer strands from the braid.

He'd spirited Mama's embroidery scissors out of her sewing box, but he hadn't yet gotten up the nerve to use them. What if this row of braids was all connected somehow like the goat bells in the garden? What if with one snip the whole decoration fell off the drapes?

Mama would kill him.

He snipped a few of the stitches holding the braid. It didn't fall off. He worked at unraveling a single cord of the twisted silk. It took a few minutes, but it could be done.

Petros wrapped one whole braid into a ball. He could unravel it later, sitting someplace where he wouldn't be taking the chance of being discovered.

He found he needed to snip a few stitches again about six inches farther along, but this was no trouble. Petros followed the broken stitches through the folds of the drapes, telling himself over and over that he would work here only a moment more. Only one more strand.

But he never stopped at one more strand. He moved to the next window and the next, and worked until the chain on the gate rattled. Petros stopped breathing for an instant. He didn't have to worry about being seen from outside—the shutters were closed. But being caught, this was a worry.

Down the hall, Papa's bare feet hit the floor and he ran along the hall and into the parlor. He crossed to a window at the other end of the room, where he could see more of the yard. Petros allowed himself a silent sigh of relief that he hadn't worked his way to that end of the room.

As Papa flipped a shutter so he could peer between the slats, Mama came to stand in the parlor doorway. "It's Elia's grandmother," Papa said in a low voice.

"I'll go," Mama said. She asked Elia's grandmother in, Papa went back to bed, and Sophie got up to go into the kitchen.

It wasn't likely Mama would come to the parlor to sit—her sofa was gone. But Petros felt relieved to hear the women settle in the kitchen. He thought about sneaking back to his room, but not very hard. He couldn't resist stealing another few minutes in the parlor.

He'd worked up a good-sized ball of cord when he heard Mama and Grandmother Lemos coming, talking in serious tones. Petros stopped pulling at the braid. He sat frozen in shock and fear as they came into the parlor.

Only now did this plan appear to have serious flaws. He hadn't thought things through properly. If he was discovered now, with so much blue braid balled up in his lap, Papa would make it that he couldn't sit down for days.

Worse, his mother might never forgive him. He might be

made to sleep in the shed with Old Mario, whose breath filled the room as he snored.

Grandmother Lemos talked of the changes in the parlor as if she spoke of the dead. Mama said she couldn't use the room since the soldiers had handled her things. Sophie called out that she'd poured the lemonade. Mama and Grandmother Lemos went back to the kitchen. Petros wasn't discovered. He made up his mind to be especially nice to Sophie when he had the chance.

He didn't move. He couldn't leave the room just yet. While the women were drinking lemonade, they might look toward the parlor and see him leaving it. Best to remain where he was.

He snipped away at the next few stitches. He pulled at the braid, being careful not to make the drapes quiver, nothing anyone might notice. After several minutes, he had another ball sizable enough to stuff into his pants pocket. Still the braid, the fringe, looked no different.

When Petros had several more inches of the cord he needed, he wrapped it around the ball he'd already begun. He moved on to another area in the fringe. Every so often, Petros scooted along the cool marble floor to the next window. He sang a whispered little song under his breath as he worked.

From the space of three windows, he made half a dozen small balls. The sight of them filled his heart with happiness. All of them unraveled and spooled together would make one fine ball of kite string.

But one more would make it finer.

Petros began a new ball. He heard the faraway rumble of a truck, hardly noticing it, really. The ball had grown a bit before he realized there couldn't be only one truck. It took several trucks traveling together to make such a noise. His heart beat faster at the thought.

Petros couldn't see through the shutters. When the trucks didn't pass but stopped in front of his house, he was glad he couldn't be seen from the outside.

He snipped his thread, hoping to make his escape unseen.

The lemonade glasses clattered. Hurried footsteps moved along the hallway. His mother's small scream startled him. Petros could taste his stomach acid—it burned his throat.

The weight of booted feet hit the veranda.

Someone pounded on the door. *BAM BAM BAM*.

chapter 36

Petros didn't move.

Papa shouted that everyone should remain in their beds.

The front door opened, and before his father could say another word, the soldiers were inside. One soldier's voice was low, but as hard and cold as the marble floor. Petros could understand little of what he said.

Another voice firmly made himself understood with excellent Greek, telling the family to go into the kitchen. To stay there. Petros tried to quiet the pounding of the blood in his ears.

Again he had only the warning tramp of boots before the drapes were thrown back from a nearby window and a fist knocked open the shutters. Light broke through, bright harsh light. The German soldier saw him then, still hidden behind the drapes. Petros felt the soldier saw everything—the strand of cord dangling from the fringe, the balls in his lap.

And Petros saw too.

The clean, smooth look of his uniform, like it was made of something other than cloth, the road dust hadn't touched it.

The large gun he wore at his hip. He carried a short stick of some kind with a leather loop on the end. And his eyes, they flashed like sunlight on water.

This was the commander.

Neither he nor Petros moved. Petros didn't even breathe. The faintest smile touched the corners of the commander's mouth. And then he winked.

Petros's whole being felt a greater shock than he'd once gotten from a battery, and that had knocked him clear across the shed. The commander reached behind the drape to give the shutters beside Petros a thump with the heel of his hand and they too opened wide.

Several soldiers stood gathered at the gate, but none were on the veranda. The commander had opened these shutters. So that Petros—this seemed hard to believe—might escape before he was discovered by Mama?

Petros gathered his shirt around the balls in his lap as the commander turned away and pointed with his stick. "Put the bed there, desk there. I'll arrange the rest," he said in too-perfect Greek that reminded Petros of the English family, the Walkers. It was the Greek of newcomers who meant to stay.

The commander said more in German, probably repeating what he'd said in Greek so his men would understand him. Petros heard this as he fled the window. He leaped off the side of the veranda, getting some nasty scratches from the bloodred roses his mother favored.

Ignoring the sting of the scratches, he walked around the

corner of the house as if he'd been directed to do so. Not one of the soldiers at the gate reacted.

Petros started running.

He ran and dropped to the ground behind the well, breathing heavily. Petros listened for any further sound from the house.

And thought of Lambros.

Below him, by at least fifty or sixty feet, Lambros knew nothing of the changes occurring above. He was safe. So long as no one took an interest in Petros, Lambros would continue to be safe there.

Petros tucked his shirt into his pants and stuffed the balls down the front. If he crawled toward the garden, he'd be hidden from the house. So he crawled for a little time on hands and knees, but the gravel bruised his knees.

He stood and ran for the grape arbor. Reaching the safety of the arbor, he listened to the mix of voices coming from the house, nothing alarming. Perhaps no one had noticed he wasn't there. He pulled the rock aside and put the balls of cord next to the mulberry juice. He slid the rock back into place.

Petros gave in to his desire to run back to the house and see what was going on. He followed Old Mario inside, the old man muttering curses meant to rain upon German heads.

"He speaks Greek," Petros said into the good hairy ear, and the curses stopped.

The commander walked through the house as if he owned it, or at least had to memorize it. He looked out at the yard from each window. Before leaving the room, he took a piece of furniture for his own: a dresser belonging to Papa.

A young soldier was told to take care of it. He scooped up a handful of shirts, emptying a drawer, but the commander saw his careless manner and stopped it. He pointed to the bed, and the soldier began to put things down there neatly. This much Petros saw as he stood in the hallway. Mama grabbed Petros and held on to him as if he were a small boy.

The commander never looked at Petros, probably on purpose, although Petros couldn't be sure. It was as Zola said, the boys knew nothing about him. They'd have to learn something of his habits, figure him out. Although he'd done Petros a kindness, he hadn't come as a friend.

Crates of wine were placed in the root cellar, to be poured only for the commander and his guests. "Guests?" Sophie whispered. "What guests?"

Papa answered. "He's a colonel. Other officers may come to visit."

"A colonel," Zola repeated, not so much to inform as to impress. Petros was already impressed, and was nearly tempted to tell Zola what the man had done.

The commander's desk was carried in, his bed set up. His books were unpacked and put on Mama's shelves. Old Mario and Zola were sent out to pick vegetables for soldiers to eat.

There were more insults to come.

The commander asked Sophie to bring him a coffee and

settled himself on the veranda. She stomped off to the kitchen, causing Mama to tighten her grip on Petros.

An odd iron-bar arrangement was pounded into the ground between one of the persimmon trees and Papa's treasured pear. No one could imagine what this was for.

When the soldiers got back into the trucks and drove away, they left the parlor ready for the commander. Papa herded Petros and the others into the kitchen.

It was a little dizzying. They'd expected this for days and now it was done, at the worst possible moment for the family's safety—when Lambros was in the well. And yet they felt safe enough, they weren't threatened at that moment. It left them with very little to say.

Although the parlor door stood closed and the hallway empty, Papa shut the kitchen door as well. Mama poured the rest of the coffee for him.

As the family sat at the table, little by little, beginning with whispers, they discovered how to be together in a house that was no longer just theirs. "What of Lambros?" Zola said under his breath.

"He won't come out until he hears three stones drop into the water," Old Mario said.

"Good plan," Papa said.

"I can't take credit for it," Old Mario said. "The boy has learned a great deal about going to war."

chapter 37

The commander knocked on the kitchen door some time later, waiting for permission to enter. Papa opened it as formally as if it were the locked front gate.

"Good evening, family," the man said. "It's my hope you will feel free to use your veranda. That you use the remainder of your house freely. I'll shut the door to my room so I may remain private. I expect to open the shutters for the light when I am at home."

Petros glanced at Mama. The commander used the words *at home*. Her distrustful face didn't change. The same couldn't be said for Sophie, whose mouth fell open like a baby bird waiting for a worm.

"About your meals . . . ," Papa said.

"I'll eat what your family eats."

Papa cleared his throat but didn't ask the question uppermost in Petros's mind. The commander answered it anyway. "In my room."

The commander looked them over, gathered at the table, as if he were memorizing them the way he had the house.

"Place a tray on a small table I'll set outside the door. That's how we'll arrange it."

Mama spoke up. "If there's no meat?"

"I don't demand meat," he said. "Please be comfortable to serve what you will." Before he closed the parlor door, he set a lamp table outside.

Mama put vegetables in the oven, then stood over a pot of rice pudding, stirring. "When he goes out, how will we know when to expect him back?"

Papa said, "He's not a guest. He won't tell us what to make of his comings and goings."

Mama put her hands on her hips, ready to argue. "How am I to know when he wants to eat?"

"We'll make a plate and cover it with a towel if he misses a meal," Papa said. "This is probably a matter of giving us no warning, of being sure we can give no one else any information ahead of time."

Mama's eyes looked wild. "Do you think the Germans suspect us?"

"I think they must suspect everyone equally," Papa said. "Except for those they suspect more. We, however, are above suspicion, being right under the commander's nose."

Zola set the first tray on the lamp table an hour later and closed the kitchen door again.

Over their evening meal of roasted vegetables and cheese, Sophie complained and Zola teased Petros over nothing at all.

Mama scolded and Papa glared when the scolding didn't take. Fifi sat on the top back step, looking in, and the dog lay flat under the table. Soon the family felt much as if the commander were not there at all.

After dinner Petros was reminded.

Papa said, "The boys and I will do the dishes, Mama. You and Sophie go out to the veranda, take the air. You must accept the commander's invitation to be in your home."

Mama's fingers trembled, but Sophie assumed an air of injury and indignation, usually saved for Petros or Zola. "It's our house," she said firmly, "and our veranda."

She left the kitchen, letting the door swing open, and Mama followed her.

The dog came out from under the table, hoping to get some scraps. Old Mario gave him a couple of parings from the cheese.

Papa spoke to Petros and Zola in a low voice. "Your cousin must stay where he is, of course. For the safety of everyone, he must not try to leave."

Petros said, "All night? Papa, he'll freeze."

"I hope he's hardier than that," Papa said. "We'll try to bring him out. But everything will depend on—" He finished with a nod of his head. "Tonight he's better off below."

"How can we warn him?" Zola asked.

"Petros will have to do it," Papa said.

"He's too little," Zola said. "Let me."

"The commander will ask where you are if you're gone for an hour," Papa said. "No, you'll join Old Mario and me in a card game. But the commander must believe he also knows where Petros is, even when he's out of sight."

"You can't go on treating me like a child," Zola said.

"Ssh." This warning came from Old Mario.

"I'm treating you like a man," Papa said quietly, and Zola's neck flushed red. Petros felt apologetic, as if he'd been shorter only to thwart Zola's desire to be a hero. "You'll leave a sack for Petros at the far wall of the property. Because of this, your brother won't have so far to crawl dragging a sack."

Papa reached for sliced bread and cheese to make Lambros a few sandwiches. Petros popped a crust into his mouth to comfort an uneasy rumble in his middle.

When Zola said, "I can do it," he looked like he'd grown a few more inches.

Papa said, "Petros, you must go through the orchard as if you're playing. Once you get past the arbor, start crawling alongside the wall to look for the sack."

Petros felt something like the charge from a battery running through his veins—part fear, but also excitement. Almost the same as when the boys had dropped Zola's messages.

Old Mario began wrapping the sandwiches in one of Mama's dish towels, saying, "No paper, no noise." He pointed to the rice pudding.

"When your mama worries," Papa said, "she likes to have sweets." He put several dishes on a platter. "Zola, take the dessert out to the veranda. And Zola," Papa said, "when you say the words 'the commander,' say them respectfully."

Zola looked as willful as Sophie, but he caught himself and said, "All right, Papa." He carried the rice puddings away, head held high.

Papa said, "When you start crawling, Petros, be patient. Stay low and keep going until you find the sack."

"Yes, Papa."

"From there you can crawl straight to the well."

Zola came back to report, "He's sitting a little apart from Mama and Sophie. He likes rice pudding. No one's speaking, otherwise."

Old Mario said to Papa, "Go out there before the commander begins to ask himself why all the men are in the kitchen."

Papa hesitated, then left them.

"First, don't look Zola's way at all," Old Mario said to Petros.

Zola had already begun packing the meal. He said, "Then, when you're hidden from anyone looking out from the veranda, you stop playing and crawl."

Old Mario said, "Keep an ear open for one of the Omeros boys. They patrol the road at night."

"And keep your head down when you're crawling," Zola added. "The moon is bright tonight."

Petros wanted suddenly to tell Zola he'd gotten the kite string. Of how the commander had helped him get the string. But he couldn't tell, not while Old Mario stood beside them.

"Papa would've chosen you to go to the well, Zola," Petros said in a whisper, "if you weren't so tall. You're a man."

"I have never been a better one than I am being just now." Zola looked a little grim.

chapter 38

"Are you ready?"

Petros nodded.

The dog followed them out the back door. Zola walked away from the back of the house, moving quickly into the shadow of the chicken house. His dog went with him but was sent back a minute later.

Fifi was grazing on the tufts of grass growing near the well. To Old Mario, Petros said, "There's one problem we haven't solved."

Old Mario said, "I know how to manage her." He pulled a packet of cigarette tobacco out of his pocket. Fifi came to him right away.

Petros said, "She smokes?" and Old Mario laughed.

"She likes a nibble of tobacco," he said. "Put a rope around her neck while I give her some."

Fifi didn't even try to bite them. Together, Petros and Old Mario walked toward the veranda. The commander sat on the far side, near the trellis, smoking.

There was a little talk as Old Mario climbed the steps, during which Petros wandered off into the orchard. He felt the

German officer's attention in a spot between his shoulder blades, but he didn't look back even once. He climbed into a tree in clear sight of the veranda, only so high that his legs could be seen dangling.

From his leafy perch, he saw the red glow of the tip of one cigarette. He thought it was odd that Papa and Old Mario didn't smoke, then realized he'd know the commander this way.

Petros dropped from the tree, swung on a low-hanging branch of the next one, and stopped behind the third. He waited there, breathing hard, before going on, tree to tree, trying to imitate his own meandering walk on so many evenings before this one.

Zola was carrying the burlap sack to the end of a faraway row of vegetables. In his mind's eye, Petros saw Zola set the sack in the dirt, then hurry back to the house. "You and Lambros must stay on the far side of the well so you can't be seen from the house," Papa had said.

Petros said, "What if he wants to run away?"

"We won't know the men who come for him. Lambros must be here to meet them."

Petros had not thought of this. "How can we be sure Lambros will know them?"

"He'll know the things they say to each other," Papa said.

Petros nodded.

"Drop the stones," Papa said. "Speak to Lambros as he climbs, but softly." His face tightened with concern. "And don't stay long. Are you sure you can manage?"

"I'm sure," Petros answered. A lie.

If no one went to the well, Lambros would wait. If he stayed down there all night, he might grow sick from the cold. This thought carried Petros deeper into the orchard.

Finally he could see only the light in the kitchen. The house blended into the night. He began to run.

A few minutes later he was on his hands and knees in the dry soil. The sharp smell of the tomatoes and basil marked the distance he'd made as he brushed against the plants.

He crawled past the garlic and the peppers and the eggplant. He passed the tomatoes, rows of them dug into trenches so the stems didn't stand as high as the eggplant. Petros dropped to his belly and dug his knees and elbows into the dirt, slithering along until his hand landed on the sack.

He inched backward to the rows of eggplant. Still, he was careful to stay low, finally reaching the row he knew would take him to the back of the well.

He could crawl on his knees here, which was faster and easier. There wasn't enough space between the rows to drag the sack at one side of him. He crawled a few steps, reached between his knees and yanked the sack out in front of him.

The tops of the eggplant bushes were just about level with the flat of his back. He wanted very much to look over them. He kept his head down anyway. The row stretched ahead of him, much longer at night and on his knees than when he walked through it by day.

When he finally reached the last eggplant bush, he flattened himself to the ground. They'd been mistaken about how well hidden he might be. He had a distance to crawl between the garden and the well, and he could be seen—

Petros could see a red dot at the edge of the veranda. He watched as the cigarette was tossed away and lay in the graveled yard. A match was struck and another cigarette lit from another place on the veranda. Papa.

Petros thought he saw a movement in the shadows of the veranda. He watched, thinking he might have imagined it, and then the other cigarette tip disappeared. Petros stared at the blank slate of his mind and the answer came quickly.

The commander had moved away, so Papa had turned away with his cigarette. Petros was safe for the moment.

He checked the moon and waited for a cloud to dim that light a little. The cloud drifted slowly. But he gathered up the sack so it might be carried across the gravel in one arm, rather than dragged.

Finally the cloud covered the moon. Petros crawled out of the cover of the leafy eggplants. The gravel hurt a lot, but Petros thought only of making nearly silent progress.

The gravel stretched away from the well for several yards. Petros rose to make a crouched run at the well. He came up against it hard, the sack falling next to his feet.

The well from one side to the other could fill a room, so he was safely out of sight and could move around a little. The danger lay in getting Lambros out of the well. Looking up, Petros made certain he'd come up behind the buckets when he stood.

The cold air met him when he hitched up onto the wall. His heart went out to poor Lambros, who had been in the well for so many hours. Petros dropped three rocks into the well, waiting to hear each one plop into the water.

He waited and, when he heard nothing, scooped up three more rocks. One. Two. Three.

After the last one splashed down, a faint sound rose from inside the well, Lambros stepping into a bucket. Petros answered this with a hiss, a warning to be silent.

The well workings creaked, taking Lambros's weight.

Petros was afraid this would be heard at the house—such sounds carried easily on the night air.

chapter 39

Lambros had to climb slowly, carefully. But after the first complaining noises from the buckets, there was almost nothing to hear. Only the slight shift in the buckets told Petros Lambros was climbing.

It felt like forever until he saw his cousin's head appear out of the dark center. "Stay on this side," he whispered. "Away from the house. The German commander is there."

Lambros didn't appear to be disturbed by this news. In fact, he didn't speak even as he dropped with hardly a sound into the gravel beside Petros.

Petros handed over the sack. "I couldn't come before now."

"What kind of sandwiches?" Lambros asked with a grin.

"Roasted peppers and cheese, I think."

Lambros made a sound of approval. "I got worried when no one turned on the well. Is everyone safe?"

"Yes."

"Where's the German now?"

"On the veranda with Papa and Old Mario."

"What's his rank?"

"Colonel."

Lambros's eyebrows made him look like Stavros, despite his beard. "Amphissa is a pin on a German map."

Petros hadn't thought of this. Papa had had such a map—before burning it. He'd marked the cities where the Allies could be found with Mama's straight pins.

Lambros was shivering, Petros realized.

"Are you wet? I thought that tunnel was dry."

"There's a trickle of water, but I sit on one side of it and rest my feet on the other. I'm dry enough."

"Where's the jacket?"

"It's kept me warm, little cousin, don't worry. But I can't wear it and climb quietly. Any word from Uncle Spiro?"

"Old Mario says we must give him another day," Petros said. "Papa wants you to remain below."

"Someone put some candles and matches in this sack."

"Old Mario."

"Tell him I'm grateful. The dark and cold will be more bearable."

"You should sit here until you're warm to the bone. Zola will have locked the gate by now, so unless trucks come, there's only the one German to worry about." Even though they hadn't planned what to do if things went wrong, Petros added, "If he leaves the house, I'll set the goats loose and make a big fuss over getting them back in."

"Go back, then," Lambros said. "Your papa's worried enough."

"I can sit with you awhile longer."

"I'll wait until I hear more stones falling into the well

before I come up again," Lambros said. He squeezed Petros's arm in a friendly good-bye. "Until tomorrow."

Petros made sure no cigarettes glowed on the veranda. As he crawled back to the orchard, he chose the best place to leave the garden. He wanted it to look as if he'd been playing there all along. He stood up on the hidden side of a pistachio tree. When he left the cover of the tree, he leaped up to hang from a branch and swung his legs as if he'd been sitting up there.

He started back to the house, not in a straight line but in a wandering way. His knees wanted to wobble a little. Exactly the way Sophie had complained of feeling when she sang in school last year. Nerves, she called it, when she was afraid of doing badly.

Petros began to run a zigzag path, touching each tree he passed as if it were a game of tag. He saw Papa stand up from his chair. Petros stopped running at the gate, breathing heavily enough to disguise any nerves he still had. He went over to the odd pair of bars, one higher than the other, that the German soldiers had pounded into the ground.

"Tomorrow morning," the commander said in a low voice from the veranda, "I'll show you what it's for."

Petros kicked a fallen unripened persimmon around the corner of the house. Perhaps there were more. Tomorrow morning he would bring Fifi to eat them, so he wouldn't look eager.

A bird murmured in the tree as Petros walked on.

"I can shoot two birds with one stone," Petros called over his shoulder. This sounded bold, daring even, except that his voice shook.

chapter 40

First thing in the morning, Petros unlocked the gate and led Fifi over to the trees. There were only a few fallen fruits, but she didn't count. She ate them.

In the trees there were several catbirds, gray, but smaller than Mama's doves. Sometimes these birds arrived in time to eat ripe fruit, but it just as often happened they came early, before the fruit was ready.

The birds were spoiled by the easy life, Petros thought. They plucked fruit and dropped it when it wasn't sweet, wasting something they might have eaten happily a week or so later.

But then he remembered the Italian soldiers, taking green tomatoes. The catbirds were hungry. He'd ask if he could throw some chicken feed on the ground for them. Probably Papa could spare the feed more easily than the fruit the birds were spoiling.

The commander came outside in something like underwear, to stretch, to swing from one iron bar to the other so he made circles in the air.

Petros tried not to look overly interested, but he didn't

refuse when the commander offered to let him hang from the bar. Petros showed off, hanging upside down.

"Can your friends do that?" the commander asked him.

Petros nodded. Everyone could hang upside down from the branch of a tree without falling.

The commander showed him how to walk on his hands.

It took Petros a couple of hard thumps onto his back to get the hang of it, but he was delighted once he could do it. "No one else can walk upside down."

"They'll learn," the commander told him, "but you'll be the first."

Mama came to look for Petros, calling in a voice sharp with fear. The commander patted him on the head, plainly trying to make Mama feel he was safe.

Fifi followed Petros into the house and was chased out the kitchen door. The whole family had gathered in there. Mama put the commander's breakfast tray on the table in the hall and shut the kitchen door.

"What did he say to you?" Zola asked very quietly.

"I may swing on the bar as often as I like," Petros said, seeing Fifi sit down in the doorway. "He walks on his hands—did you see him?"

"Shah," Mama said. "He's not an entertainment."

A knock sounded, and Papa opened the kitchen door.

The commander stood there. Seeing Mama's concern, he said to Papa, "Herr, I think we can agree. Wars should be fought among men, not boys. Boys have to grow up. Even in war, boys play."

A great many arguments crossed Papa's face, but he only nodded.

"That's all, then," the commander said. "Breakfast looks very good, Mrs., thank you." Papa didn't close the kitchen door until the commander had closed the parlor door.

Petros reached for his glass of milk, suddenly thirsty. Boys played. But it was also necessary to learn things about the commander. They wouldn't send any more messages, but the war effort wouldn't end, would it? Looking at his brother, he saw in Zola's eyes it wouldn't.

Even the way Zola then said, "We must remember to take a can when we go to the tomato plants. Yesterday I saw caterpillars to be picked off them," was a kind of lie. If Zola was picking caterpillars, he was going to make them carry letters like pigeons.

This thought made Petros laugh suddenly, laugh so hard milk shot up into his nose. He coughed and had to be clapped hard on the back. The dog barked and Fifi stood as if a game was about to begin.

The commander left shortly after eating his breakfast. The family heard him go out, that was all. Mama twisted her apron around her hands. "Work near the house today."

"Haven't I waited until he was gone?" Papa said.

After this, breakfast was much the same as always, with teasing and scolding as part of the menu. The morning was different only because Papa remained at the table longer.

"Enough talk," Old Mario said. "We must go drag that boy out of the well for an hour or two in the sun. He'll have turned blue by now."

Sophie looked out the window as she washed the dishes. "Where will we hide Lambros?"

"In the garden," Mama said. "If he's wearing a hat, looking down to pull weeds, no one will see him."

A little later, Petros carried a basket of tomatoes and basil to the house. Mama was cleaning the commander's room, running a mop over the floor.

Sophie stood at the doorway and pointed to a picture in a frame. "Mama's to touch nothing on a desk or table, not even to dust. But look there, next to his bed. They have families."

Petros saw the commander and his wife and two boys his own age or younger. "Everyone has a family," he said, although he saw Sophie's point. It was sometimes hard to remember this was true.

Mama said, "Tell Zola to start more seeds this morning. The commander asked your father to take more vegetables into town. If we're to feed some of his men as well as the families we provide for, we need more rows."

When Petros found him, Zola said, "If I'm out of sight planting seeds, and Lambros takes my place in the garden, anyone passing will think it's me out there with Papa and Old Mario."

chapter 41

Zola went straight to the shed. Petros dropped three stones into the well, and while he stood around the front gate, ready to shout a hello if anyone came into sight, Lambros climbed out. When Papa called Petros back, Lambros was already in among the beans, soaking up the sun.

Fifi followed Petros like she was his personal dog. Once, before he'd realized she was there, she ate a row of his new pepper plants, leaving him only Mr. Katzen's pepper.

When he shooed her away, she ran off kicking her heels up high, looking so pleased with herself, he had to forgive her.

He turned back to the garden and noticed Elia across the road, watching him.

Petros felt torn. He couldn't invite Elia over because Lambros was picking beans. And he couldn't risk that Elia would come looking for him in the evening either. Petros didn't wave and Elia didn't wave. And Elia didn't walk across the road. This was good, on the one hand, but also troubling.

Petros found Zola hunched over his small pots in the shed. "Elia doesn't wave when he sees me."

Zola didn't look up. "The commander's living here and everyone is afraid of him. Elia's father probably told him he can't come over here anymore."

"The Lemos family knew this would happen."

"And now it has," Zola said. "His car stops here every day, and trucks filled with his men, too. If he were staying somewhere else, those soldiers would pass by without stopping."

"Aren't the other officers staying in somebody's house?"

"Yes. Probably those people don't have any friends stopping by either," Zola said, and stood up straight. Stretched. "But we are a bigger problem to the Lemos family. We have something to hide."

"Lambros."

"Us. I mean us." Zola frowned. "Papa said if he were Lemos and his friends across the road were American, he'd tell his children to stay home. He'd be afraid for his own family first."

"If the people across the road had trouble, Papa would help," Petros said. "Mama too."

Zola sounded almost angry when he said, "We don't want the Lemos family wondering who *is* that extra fellow in the garden. We don't want their help."

"If something goes wrong," Petros said, "how will you know when Lambros goes into the well?"

"Old Mario has a scarf wrapped around his scalp. He'll put on the hat Lambros is wearing."

Talking with Zola, Petros hadn't really noticed the other

sound in his ears. Not until the car pulled up outside the gate with a shriek of brakes and Zola dropped to the dirt floor.

Petros saw the commander getting out of his car. He'd gone away with a driver but he was alone now. Petros saw Lambros put down his basket. "Stay here," he told Zola.

Petros ran toward the commander, pulling his slingshot out of his pocket. "I can kill two birds with one stone!"

"That would be pretty good shooting," the commander said.

"I did it this morning," Petros said with bravado. A lie. "I can do it again now."

"All right. Let's see it."

Petros ran to the far side of the veranda, behind the leafy trellis, where the well couldn't be seen. The commander followed him.

"This is the stone," Petros said, digging it out of his pocket. In the back of his mind, Petros saw Zola run from the shed to the garden. How long would it take for Lambros to hide?

"See? It's my lucky stone." He showed it off as if it were one of Papa's card tricks.

"Let us hope so," the commander said, smiling.

Petros felt a stirring of shame in his heart. The commander had been good to him so far. To his family. He had come as the enemy and made himself one of two men, the way Uncle Spiro thought of them.

But the other man, Lambros, was Petros's cousin.

"See that bird?" Petros pointed to a finch on the vine-covered trellis. Not an easy shot. The finches were quick, but he didn't allow this thought to settle. He kept his eye on the bird.

He set the stone, drew back, and shot.

It was a lucky shot—he knew that immediately. The finch was used to people. It turned away, and in an instant it fell to the veranda.

"One bird," Petros shouted, and a few of the finches flew away.

The commander laughed. "You said two."

Petros ran up onto the veranda and retrieved the stone. He held it out. "Two birds with this one stone."

Another laugh. "Very tricky," the commander said.

Petros pointed to the persimmon tree. "Two birds in a row."

As they neared the trees, the well stood in the distance behind them. Petros didn't look there but danced ahead, trying to be everything at once—convincing as a boy at play, and more interesting than whatever had brought the commander back when no one expected him.

A catbird with its face in the fruit was the target he hoped for. These birds were a sure kill. One lifted into the air at his approach, and although it wasn't the easy target Petros meant to find, the lucky stone wanted it.

Petros placed the stone while moving, drew, and shot, never hoping for another lucky shot, not even caring if he failed, imagining the chill darkness closing around Lambros, the safety of the well.

The stone found its mark.

The catbird fell to the ground.

"Very good," the commander said as proudly as Papa might, clapping his hands together. "You're a good shot."

As proudly as Papa. The thought struck Petros as soundly in his guilty heart as the stone did the bird. "I have a lucky stone," he said.

The commander crossed his arms over his chest.

Mama saved Petros further embarrassment, coming out on the veranda. She said to the commander, "To eat?" as if the man hadn't already spoken perfectly fine Greek to them. At the same time, she put her hand out to Petros, the picture of a mama looking for help.

"No, Mrs. I only came back for some papers. I'm going right out again." She gave the commander a stiff little nod and gathered Petros to her as he stepped up on the veranda.

He felt the tremble in her hand on his shoulder. He went inside, Mama only a step behind him. "Go to the kitchen," she said.

Petros had begun to appreciate how Mama would get through this, holding the commander, even the danger, at a distance. Petros thought at least she would never have a guilty heart.

chapter 42

Either the sack was heavier tonight or Petros's arms were weary from hanging on the bar. He couldn't decide which. When one arm grew tired with pulling the sack forward, he switched to the other. It took him longer to reach the well, he thought.

When Petros dropped three stones, it was with a great sense of relief. Lambros came out of the well shivering, more than before.

"Uncle Spiro's sitting on the veranda," Petros said to give Lambros time to warm up. "After Old Mario introduced him, no one talked."

Lambros said, "Perhaps your papa and Uncle Spiro can't figure out how to start a conversation after so many years."

That Uncle Spiro had come at all said everything.

"Mama's feeding him there." Uncle Spiro had come late, probably deliberately. It wasn't troubling to lack conversation on the veranda, but it would have been strange at the kitchen table.

"What do you think of the commander?" Lambros asked. His voice sounded steadier—he'd warmed up a little.

"He walks on his hands."

Lambros raised his eyebrows.

"For a little time in the morning. He has a name for it, I forget. He hangs from a bar and swings like a monkey."

"He's a gymnast."

"He has two sons. You'd like him if it wasn't for this war."

"I don't doubt it," Lambros said.

"I never imagined him having a family."

"It never helps to think of that," Lambros said.

Petros agreed. Because his next thought had been *What if he dies?* Everyone worried when they thought of Lambros, and it never helped. Of course they also bragged about his courage. But even that was a kind of worry.

Lambros said, "You did a fine job of turning the commander's attention today."

"I tricked him."

"You kept us all safe," Lambros said. "You did right. You did a man's job. But you must remember to go on being a boy. That's your job if there are no more such emergencies."

Petros warmed like a lantern.

"Lambros, the Georges told us you held off the Italians for six days. Single-handedly."

"I had the company of five mules. Don't sell them short."

"You climbed the Needle bare-handed. No one did that before."

Lambros said, "Perhaps no one was that scared before."

"And you escaped the Gestapo."

"When it's time to sleep, the Germans sleep. When it's time to get together in a meeting, they go. This much was on my side," Lambros said. "But I was lucky too. Very lucky."

"I hope I'm so lucky," Petros said.

"I pray you never have to be," Lambros said.

"How do you account for it? Did you know you would succeed?"

"I knew only what I faced if I didn't."

"Everyone before you knew the same thing," Petros said. "How did you become such a good fighter?"

Lambros said, "Do you remember that time you cut your foot badly and I fainted at the sight of blood?"

"Yes."

"I no longer faint. But I don't look too closely."

Petros let this sink in. "Do you speak to the dead?"

Lambros cocked his head, but it was too dark for Petros to read the look on his face. "Sometimes they speak to me. It would be rude to ignore them, don't you think?"

"Who are these dead?"

"Too many." Together they listened to the night for a time. Fifi, tied inside the goat pen, bleated. Lambros said, "You should get back."

"I can wait."

"I'm going with Uncle Spiro, Petros."

Petros didn't know why someone else hadn't come for Lambros, a man who could fight off a German soldier. One of those men who had come into the kitchen, someone a little scary. "Didn't Uncle Spiro tell someone else to come and help you get past the Germans?"

"He'll have told someone to feed his chickens," Lambros said.

"It's past curfew," Petros said. "Uncle Spiro didn't worry between his farm and ours, but what about when you get further away?"

"Those Omeros boys have a few tricks up their sleeves," Lambros said.

"Really?" Petros wouldn't have suspected it.

"They're smarter than they look," Lambros said, the white of his teeth flashing a little in the moonlight when he grinned. "Also, their grandmother has been my grandmother's friend since they were little girls together. We are almost as good as cousins."

Lambros ran his fingers through Petros's hair and added, "Almost."

Petros knew he should go, and yet he felt something had been left unsaid. "Mama's mother, you know her?"

"Popi."

"She speaks to the dead," Petros said. "She says they don't talk to just anyone."

"Your grandmother's right."

"They don't talk to me."

"Someday, Petros," Lambros said, "when you need them, that's when they'll speak to you."

As Petros crawled back through the garden, he heard the creak of Uncle Spiro's donkey cart passing him. The soft burr of Uncle Spiro's voice in a low song.

It was then the understanding came. For a stranger, Uncle Spiro would have sent someone else. For those he loved, no one else would do.

Petros flipped over in his bed again. He couldn't sleep. He felt like he'd been lying awake in the dark for hours. He wished the time had already come when he might know Lambros had arrived wherever Uncle Spiro was taking him.

Uncle Spiro too. This waiting bothered Petros a great deal.

"How did you think of what to do?" Zola said to him. "When the commander came, you thought fast."

"No, I moved fast," Petros said.

"So?"

"It didn't feel like thinking," Petros said. "It was as if the dead whispered in my ear, Here's what to do. I didn't have to think at all." He felt a little thrill at realizing this.

"You did well."

"Do you think Lambros is safe tonight?"

"Uncle Spiro's a magician," Zola said.

"A magician?"

"All those card tricks Papa knows," Zola said. "Who do you think taught him?"

It made sense that Papa had gone to his little brother for help. Petros decided he could sleep after all.

Three days later Uncle Spiro stopped his cart at the gate. Petros saw him and ran to him. Still, Papa got there first. Uncle Spiro said to him, "The boy's well. Our sister sends you her love."

chapter 43

Petros spent a few minutes hanging from the bar after he unlocked the gate the next morning. It made his wrists ache. This would be worth it if one day he could do as the commander did, swinging from one bar to the other and back again.

When the commander came out, Petros went inside with a little nod. In the kitchen, plans were already made for a trip into town. Papa, Old Mario, and Zola had gone out to the garden to pick vegetables. Mama said, "Petros, pick all your tomatoes. We'll need them to fill the baskets."

Petros carried a piece of fried bread out to the garden with him. The broken pepper plant had put all its labors into one pepper. It was growing the biggest pepper he'd ever seen.

A breeze fluttered through the green pepper leaves.

He worked for a time, holding himself aloft with memories of the days the boys had run mad through the village, tossing a sand ball back and forth.

When he heard footsteps, he looked up from the smell of baked earth and bruised leaves to see the commander standing at the edge of his garden. He jerked a little, a reflex.

"I didn't mean to frighten you," the commander said.

Perhaps Petros was frightened. He wasn't sure.

"What happened to this pepper plant?" the commander asked him.

"It met with an accident," Petros said. "But I'm giving it a chance."

"Good," the commander said. "I like that you aren't wasteful."

Petros ducked his head. He had Mr. Katzen to thank for this undeserved compliment. "I'll save the seeds from the big pepper," Petros said. "Perhaps more of my plants will grow bigger peppers like it."

Papa came along then and said, "We're ready."

"I want to introduce you to a few people," the commander said. "Then you'll be able to come to the command post without alarming anyone. More important, perhaps, without anyone alarming you."

Papa looked resigned.

"Are you taking the boys?" the commander asked him.

"Only Petros," Papa said.

Petros sat between Papa and Old Mario in the truck. Behind the seat several dozen eggs were packed in straw with a blanket thrown over them. They were for families, not for soldiers.

First Papa stopped at the school building, now called the command post. Once they were relieved of more than half the vegetables on the truck, Papa and Old Mario followed their usual route.

They stopped first to leave vegetables and eggs and cheese with Auntie. Papa sent them Lambros's love. He made it sound as if Lambros had passed them running, not as if he'd spent nights belowground in their well.

Stavros frowned but said nothing.

"He couldn't come to you," Petros told him the moment Papa let the boys go to Stavros's room. "He meant to keep you safe that way."

"Perhaps. But he also meant to keep me home," Stavros said with a deep bitterness.

Against his better judgment, Petros told his secret. "I made a kite."

"No. Where is it?"

"Come out to the house—I'll show you," Petros said. "Zola helped me to hide it. I made it from the paper flag we had for the assembly. Remember it?"

"Very fine," Stavros said. "We have to make a tail worthy of it."

Papa and Old Mario were having a sweet drink with Auntie, so the boys pulled a box of money out from under her bed. They tied the bills at the middle with some fishing line Stavros had found. The tail looked like it was made of bow ties.

"But what about string?" Stavros said while they worked. There was only enough fishing line for the tail.

Petros told him where he'd gotten the kite string. He

showed the thin strand of silk he still had in his pocket, and Stavros put it into his own. They planned for him to walk out to the farm the next day.

But Petros took the kite tail with him, tucked carefully into Stavros's book bag, which was strung across Petros's back.

"Auntie checks my room lately," Stavros said. "She worries that I might try something like writing notes, since the idea has been put into my head."

At this they both laughed.

Papa made several more stops, where the vegetables and eggs were greeted like bread with honey. Most of them were given away. Then Papa swung back through the village before going home. It was said the Basilis sisters wanted to buy wheat.

Old Mario remarked on the young soldiers hanging about outside the shops. However German these soldiers were, life had to go on. Children were once more allowed to play outside. Shutters on windows hung open. The soldiers were ignored as much as possible.

Papa went into the bakery to talk business. Leaving Old Mario to wait in the truck, Petros stood near the bakery wall, but he didn't lean against it. He took care not to crush the kite tail as he watched two small boys learning to shoot marbles.

Their marbles didn't roll more than six or eight inches. One of them finally got frustrated and threw a marble, hitting one of the soldiers on the leg. Rather than get angry, the fellow got down on one knee to show the boys another way.

Petros stood with a couple of men who watched with interest. The soldier shot somewhat differently, and even the poor clay marbles went very far.

Petros envied the German's skills as the little boys ran after a speeding marble, laughing. He thought it might soon be true that the village would be comfortable with German soldiers in their midst.

Just then Papa stepped outside. He stopped there, Mama's string sack dangling from his wrist, the sack fat with two loaves of the bread no one liked.

Across the square a black car came around the corner very fast, pulling up hard at the open gate in front of Stavros's home. The soldier who was good at marbles moved quickly into the street.

Even though he was scared, Petros stepped forward too. Papa grabbed him by the shoulder with a hard grip, a warning to stand still.

Two soldiers got out of the car and ran across the yard to Stavros's house. One of the soldiers banged on the door, another kicked it so hard it flew open, and they barged inside.

There were shouts and a scream.

One soldier roughly pushed Stavros out into the street. The other followed them, controlling Auntie with one arm twisted behind her back. She kept up a strange breathless screaming.

An officer moving more slowly, importantly, got out of the car to meet them. And another, smaller officer got out on the other side of the car. The soldier was holding Stavros by the neck when they reached the street.

"Gestapo," Papa whispered as a fourth man climbed out of the car. "They're looking for Lambros."

"He's not here," Petros said in a small voice. Immediately he knew why Papa wouldn't let them speak of Lambros having been in the well, not even to Stavros.

The smaller officer spoke quietly to Auntie; Petros doubted she could even hear him. Nearby, one of the men who'd watched the marble game said, "What's the meaning of this?"

The other man said, "They're making an example of the family."

"No one has been there," the nearby man said to Papa, who nodded. "It's only the old woman and the boy."

The Gestapo officer yelled into Auntie's face, and she shook her head—no, she didn't know where Lambros was, and no, to whatever else he asked in his poor Greek.

A dog started barking.

The other officer turned to Stavros, who shook his head also, no to both questions. "Where's your brother hiding?" he shouted.

Stavros didn't answer. His brows made a shelf over his eyes, hiding whatever he felt besides anger. Auntie knew this look too and became more shrill.

"Papa," Petros said. It felt like a shout but came out as only a whisper. He noticed many other things at the same time. Papa's grip tightening. Old Mario sitting in the truck. The frozen postures of so many people standing on the street.

Only soldiers moved, first into the middle of the street, and then, when the Gestapo officer pulled a gun, away again.

Petros stopped breathing.

Stavros stayed rigid with stubbornness. Petros understood why the Gestapo officer went on yelling and yelling. But that wasn't the way to move Stavros.

Behind Petros, one of the Basilis sisters stood in the doorway, reporting the events to all who remained inside the bakery.

The Gestapo officer raised his gun to Stavros's face, shouting so continuously Stavros wouldn't have been heard if he'd answered. Auntie fought to free herself but could not.

Petros's mind went on working. On the one hand, he believed the officer would spare Stavros at the last moment—or save him somehow. But on the other hand, how could the man back down?

The commander came out of the schoolhouse, running, and some small voice within Petros cheered his speed.

The officer holding the gun shook it, warning Stavros, but then heard the commander running up behind him. He looked away from Stavros as the gun went off.

A burst of color splashed at Stavros's throat.

In the moment Stavros hit the dirt of the street, Papa clapped his hand over Petros's eyes. In the moment Stavros hit the dirt of the street, questions lit Petros's mind like flashes of lightning:

Why had the officer looked away? Was he afraid of seeing Stavros die? In the same way that Lambros used to faint at the sight of blood?

Had he only just heard the commander, and the gun went off accidentally?

Had the commander reached out and caused the gun to go off?

Petros had seen the whole thing, but his mind had begun wrapping the event in layers of questions, burying the details as deeply as Mama's Lenox china wrapped in paper and straw.

As Stavros fell, there were screams of shock all around, and people began to cry. The commander and the Gestapo officer were in a shouting match, all garbled words.

Stavros lay in the street, so still, the red stain spreading over his white shirt. This much Petros saw before Auntie threw herself over him, as if to hold his soul within.

Papa turned Petros away from the square. "Go home," he said. "Don't stop anywhere. Don't talk to anyone. Stay off the road."

"Mama?"

"Tell her, but everyone's to go into the house. No one stays in the yard or garden."

The argument going on above Stavros broke off as suddenly as the gunshot tore the air, and there was silence behind Petros. But he went, letting Papa see him as he was meant to go, obedient. He got around the corner of the bakery before he looked back.

The men who'd gotten out of the car had returned to it. The commander stood long enough to watch them drive off in a reckless manner, the black car swerving all around the village square.

The commander's back was turned to Auntie and Stavros, as if in his anger he'd forgotten them. The other soldiers appeared to ignore Auntie's wailing. It was their job to wait for orders.

Petros waited long enough to see the commander turn on his heel and stomp back toward the command post. Some soldiers followed him, others simply walked away from the street as if they had something else to do.

Papa crouched over Auntie and Stavros. Old Mario got out of the truck, hurrying in a way that had only become true of late, when speed was called for. Other people had begun to move toward them to help.

Petros ran, still seeing in his mind's eye the way Stavros lay, unmoving. Still seeing the bright blood at his throat.

chapter 44

The mile home stretched longer than it had ever been as Petros cut across one orchard and then another, through a farmyard where a dog chased him and then the Lemoses' orchard.

The sunlight cut as sharply into his eyes as scissors, and his head ached, but he ran, Stavros's book bag flopping against his back. Wave after wave of nausea made him stop to bend over, sweating, shaking. And then he ran on. And walked, and for a few minutes, crawled.

When he reached home, Mama and Sophie were on the veranda. "Who is that?" Sophie said to Mama while looking straight at him.

It seemed Mama looked for a long time as Petros clung shakily to the locked gate. He understood, remembering the look of Lambros in the well, how different he'd looked. Petros had no breath left in him to call out.

Everything happened next.

Mama shrieked and began to run at him.

And next.

"Zola!" Sophie yelled, and then began to scream.

And next.

Zola shot from the other side of the house at the sound of Mama's voice and ran to unlock the gate, having the key in his pocket.

Petros's throat tightened around any words he tried to speak. Mama grabbed him through the gate, holding him up. "What happened?" she kept saying, and finally Petros was able to say, "Stavros has been shot."

The gate swung open and Petros fell a little against Mama. Sophie clung to Mama's other side as Zola pushed him toward the house.

"What's this?" Mama asked as she tugged at the book bag. She let go of it almost immediately, asking, "Where's your father?"

"Has something happened to Papa?" Sophie cried. "I thought you were all together."

Petros didn't even try to answer. Their voices rose around him, and the dog's barking was especially sharp. It was a comfort, nearly.

The house felt cool as they entered in a clump of family bodies clinging to each other, the kitchen looked dark after his run in the white sunlight. Mama said, "Why didn't you come home with your father?" as she let him fall into a chair.

"Auntie needed him," Petros said, answering her worry. "Old Mario too," and here Petros let his head rest on the kitchen table, hot tears burning beneath his eyelids. "Stavros is dead."

There was a sudden noise at a distance, Sophie shouting, and Mama argued with Zola, who wanted to run back to town. Mama pulled Petros upright and set a cool wet cloth against his face, and the noise of his family rushed at him again.

He knew there was something else he was to say, the answer to this, but he couldn't bring it to mind. He heard the rustle of the kite tail in the book bag and leaned away from the chair.

At that moment Papa's truck came through the open gate. Zola ran outside, his dog fast behind him. Sophie ran too, getting to the door just ahead of Petros and Mama.

Papa pulled up at the steps to the kitchen.

"Mama!" Sophie cried, and covered her eyes at the sight of Old Mario in the truck bed with Stavros's bloodied body.

Sophie leaned against the door frame and slid to the floor, blocking the doorway. Mama slapped the wet towel, still in her hands, to the back of Sophie's head. "You have to get out of the way," she said, pulling at Sophie.

Zola climbed into the truck, touching Stavros's leg, and said to Petros, "He isn't dead, stupid."

"Zola!" This was Papa and Mama together.

"*I* thought he was dead," Papa said, perhaps defending Petros but also telling Mama what had happened.

Old Mario said, "It was perhaps the luckiest wound anyone

ever received. The doctor came running and stopped the bleeding. But it's only a little flesh missing."

"Get up," Mama told Sophie, pulling at her again. "You have to help Auntie." The old lady sat in the truck, weeping. Sophie dragged herself up.

"We've told her and told her he's breathing," Papa said, "but she believes Stavros is gone."

Helped by Zola, Old Mario lifted Stavros into Papa's arms. "Thanks to the doctor's quick thinking," Old Mario said, "the whole village believes he's dead."

Zola took the weight of Stavros's legs as they carried him into the house. "I'm going up to the roof," Old Mario said.

Sophie reached through the truck window. "Auntie, don't cry. Auntie, let's go into the kitchen."

They carried Stavros through the house, the dog nearly tripping them as he scurried around them. Papa ignored the dog as he said, ". . . the gun at his head. The man moved a little before he pulled the trigger, and the bullet nicked Stavros's ear. A lot of blood, but not likely to kill him."

They laid him on Zola's bed.

Mama hurried back to the kitchen, where she grabbed a handful of clean dish towels and pumped a bowl of water. Sophie came in at the kitchen, pulling Auntie along, nearly carrying her.

Petros hung back in the hallway. He wanted to help Sophie, who kept up a running stream of words in a voice that was anything but reassuring.

But he also wanted to be where Stavros was, and followed Mama back to the bedroom, where he hovered in the doorway.

Papa had stripped away the bloody clothing and covered Stavros with the sheet.

Mama soaked a towel and wrung it nearly dry to wipe the dirt off Stavros's face. This seemed to bother him, but he went on sleeping.

Zola asked, "Why doesn't he wake up?"

"The doctor gave him something to make him sleep," Papa said, sounding . . . not cheerful, but so relieved it could have been mistaken for cheerfulness. "The bleeding cleaned the wound, which is good. Only, the doctor says, maybe his hearing will suffer. Such a blast so close to the ear is bad."

Mama scolded with her tongue, a sign she would be angry over something later. Anything. Nothing.

Papa added, "He's alive, and we can't improve on that."

Zola said, "We can't hide him in the well."

Petros said, "Uncle Spiro." All of them looked at him, including Mama. "Take Stavros and Auntie to Uncle Spiro's farm," Petros said.

"It's the best we can do," Mama said, getting up. "If Stavros can travel, he should be taken to his mother." She went back to the kitchen, and Petros followed her.

Sophie and Auntie had gotten no farther than the kitchen table and waited to hear about Stavros. Mama looked alarming, Petros thought, in her bloodied apron, telling good news.

Auntie cried, but differently, as if she finally believed

Stavros lived. Despite the good news that he was in fact a lucky bird that day, Sophie remained badly upset.

"Sophie, go to your room," Mama said as she pumped clean water.

When Old Mario called down from the stairs that all remained clear on the road to the village, the fright came back to Auntie's face. Petros urged the old lady to her feet. "Auntie, come see Stavros. See what's true."

Auntie leaned on Petros, but also she pushed him ahead of her. When they reached the bedroom, Papa had taken over where Mama left off, cleaning the dirt off Stavros.

"If he's going to live," Auntie said, wearing the frown so familiar from Stavros's face, "take him to Spiro, who can take him to Hypatia. I can't see him killed again."

Mama returned from the kitchen and talked constantly as she bandaged Stavros, trying to persuade Auntie to go too, but the old lady kept saying, "No. No."

Mama sent Petros outside with shorts and two shirts for Stavros. The bottle of iodine. Papa was filling the gas tank as Zola threw buckets of water across the truck bed. Old Mario swept the blood out with a broom.

Papa sent Petros back inside. "Fold two blankets for Stavros to lie on."

It was a simple thing to do, but Sophie helped him in that big-sister way of hers. "Whose bag is this?" she asked, pulling on the book bag Petros still wore.

"It belongs to Stavros," he said. He dropped it on the table.

And as he carried the blankets outside, Sophie carried the book bag. "It weighs nothing," she said, shaking it. "What's inside?"

"Dead bugs," Petros said, and caught the bag as she dropped it.

Zola had just finished mopping up the water in the truck bed. When Sophie went back inside, he asked, "What is it really?"

"A kite tail." Petros opened the bag and showed Zola, who laughed.

Together they laid the blankets out in the truck bed. "We should send the kite with Stavros," Petros told Zola.

"All right, all right," Zola said in an irritated way.

"We don't dare fly it anyway," Petros said. "Papa would kill us for sure."

"Still, it doesn't hurt to dream," Zola said.

Petros could hardly breathe. Zola wasn't talking to him as the big brother talking to a little one. He was speaking simply as one brother to another.

Zola looked up from straightening the blanket. "What will he do for string?"

"I have string," Petros said. "I'll go get it."

Zola jumped out of the truck, going for the kite. Petros heard him on the stairs to the roof. He set the book bag next to the box of clothing, then ran to the arbor for the balls of silken string. Holding them against his chest, he ran back to the truck, where everyone was gathering.

Papa was carrying Stavros out to the truck, but it was Auntie who stood with arms lifted as if she were doing the job.

"Burn it," Papa said, having seen the kite as Zola came down the stairs. But Zola lifted the corner of the blankets, laid the kite flat, and threw the blankets back over it.

"Is it a kite?" Auntie asked. "He loves kites."

"It's nothing American," Petros said, and quickly tossed the silken balls into the box with the clothing and tomatoes. "It will make Stavros live and be well. If it doesn't get broken."

Mama's eyes sharpened at seeing the color of those balls, but she had her hands full with Auntie, who looked less lost every minute. Auntie was shouting instructions of her own as she climbed into the seat and briskly rolled down the window.

Old Mario climbed into the truck bed, helping Papa with Stavros. He placed Stavros's legs over the area where the kite was hidden. The frame was strong enough to bear that much weight, Petros felt sure.

Papa looked torn, but was distracted when Zola said, "Let me come."

Papa said, "It's your job to think Stavros is dead, as Petros thought Stavros was dead. Help your mother and sister lay out a table for mourning. That's your job."

"You're right," Zola said as Papa got behind the wheel. "I didn't think."

"It's good to know you sometimes rest from all that thinking," Papa said. "Put a hen in a burlap sack and go trade the fishmonger."

"I'll do that," Old Mario said, climbing back off the truck bed. "I'm an old man. This is too much for me. Take your grown son with you."

Papa hesitated, then nodded. Zola stepped up into the truck, his face looking sunburned but satisfied. As Papa drove away, Mama told Sophie they had to kill a few chickens.

"No one has died," Old Mario muttered. "Kill just one."

"It can't be helped," Mama said.

Petros knew Mama would have things to tell him about the table, even though they had no dead to mourn. He would simply do as he was told. He allowed himself a minute to watch the truck out of sight, the road dust beginning to settle at the front gate.

Stavros would be with Lambros—that's what he wanted most.

Across the street, Elia stepped out from behind a tree. He'd seen the whole thing, Petros thought, even if all he saw was Stavros carried out to the truck and Papa driving away.

chapter 45

Old Mario looked doubtfully at the burlap sack when he was ready to go. "What if the fishmonger wants more than one chicken?"

"Tell him his fish are dead," Mama said. "The hen lays an egg a day."

Mama's courage began to fail at thinking of how many villagers would come to the church in the village. "It's a necessary lie," she said worriedly. "But one I've begun to dread living with."

Sophie had recovered enough to help in the kitchen, but not enough to argue this with Mama. It fell to Petros to keep saying, "Everything will be fine. Fine."

He and Sophie put two tables together in the kitchen and set out as many chairs as they could lay hands on. Some of these were in the cellar. Petros made quick work of it, passing the chairs upward to Mama and Sophie and then putting the room back to rights, sliding the bed over the cellar door.

They'd just finished with this when Old Mario returned,

saying, "The fish weighs less than the chicken." He seemed to want to grumble about this some more, but the commander drove into the yard. Less than an hour after Papa had gone, which made his hasty departure wise.

The commander came into the house at the front and knocked on the kitchen door. Mama opened it, wringing her hands, real tears of fright in her eyes. Her anger rose to meet the commander. "This was a terrible thing for my son to see."

"I didn't mean for it to happen," the commander said. He tried to walk the border of being the colonel, but also he showed real sadness. "A mistake."

He almost whispered, asking, "Your husband has not returned, Mrs.?"

Mama nodded. "He's gone to tell the rest of the family." Her tears looked convincing to Petros, who remembered immediately how terrible he'd felt, running home believing Stavros had been killed.

Sophie ran to be at Mama's back.

The commander said, "I tried. I couldn't stop it."

Petros remained where he stood. Many mistakes happened, but what Petros saw was no different from the things he'd heard about over the radio. He couldn't accept this apology.

There were no tears in Sophie's eyes. In the end it may have been the hatred Sophie didn't hide that convinced the commander.

Or it may have been Elia, who came to the back door and

stood silently, waiting to be invited in. A long moment of no one speaking, no one moving, followed his appearance.

Elia's grandmother broke this silence, coming through the front door without knocking. She wore her black dress for mourning. She believed Stavros to be dead.

She put her arms around Mama, saying, "I'm sorry, I'm so sorry for your loss."

This by itself was kind and courageous. But especially the scowling look she gave the commander for bothering the bereaved family convinced him.

Mama gave Petros and Sophie a nervous glance. What could she say but what Petros had told them after running home?

Only Petros knew what Elia had seen, and even he didn't know what Elia thought of it.

Mama looked relieved to see Papa's truck turn into the yard and stop quickly, gravel spitting out from under the tires. She met him on the veranda, but the commander had already stepped outside. All she could say was said with tears.

"How's the boy?" the commander asked.

"He lived for an hour," Papa said. This was a smart lie, Petros realized, because no one in the village knew otherwise. But some people might know he hadn't died right away.

The commander apologized all over again, his voice breaking over the words *the boy's death*. For some reason, these words tore a sob from Petros's chest.

Mama did her part, pulling Petros into her arms so

forcefully he couldn't have resisted. Still, Petros felt the way the commander watched them, listened, his attention enough to take the breath away.

"I took my older son with me when I drove the body to my brother," Papa told the commander, "and I left my son there to help with his grandmother."

"About the man we're looking for . . . ," the commander began.

"Lambros has been mad since boyhood," Old Mario said. An impressive lie. "The family didn't know where he is."

Papa went on, saying, "He's been away for many years." Petros hadn't known his father or Old Mario were capable of such excellent lies. He pulled away from Mama's shoulder.

"I know the rumors," Papa said. "But it does the boy and his grandmother a great wrong to think they'd hide him. I tell you the truth, even though it endangers *my* children to anger you."

The rest of the Lemos family came across the road several minutes later, afraid still, crossing the veranda with slow steps. Luckily they didn't ask any questions, perhaps because the commander stood nearby.

"I—" the commander began.

Petros saw it in the commander's face, he wanted to be one of two men. And yet he had to remain the commander. He clicked his heels together and bowed his head a little. "I leave your family to your sorrow."

The first few minutes were awkward. The men talked among themselves in low voices, gathered in one corner of the kitchen. The women were quiet, more than was usual, even at such a sad time. No one wanted a careless word to be overheard by the commander.

Two more families came, still in work clothes. The men didn't go to the veranda but went into the garden with rakes and shovels, seeing the day's work done. The women went to the kitchen and prepared to fry the fish.

They made things ready for death as usual, if such a thing were possible. Mama and Sophie changed into old dark dresses. Petros put on a black suit that used to belong to his brother. He'd grown so tall that his wrist and ankle bones showed.

After dinner Papa and the other men sat and smoked on the veranda. There was no card game, no talk. They were noticeable only as red points of light in the darkness.

Five days later the commander informed them the officer from the Gestapo had gone back to Athens. He said it in a manner that suggested this wouldn't even interest them, and yet his eyes told a different story.

Three more days passed, little more than a week after Stavros had been carried to the mountains, and Zola came back. He whispered to each of them the news: Uncle Spiro had returned. Stavros had arrived at the mountain camp safely and was healing well.

A few weeks after that, Uncle Spiro brought Auntie to the house for a visit. "Hello," he called out. Auntie wore her black, but then, she had been dressed for mourning for years.

Uncle Spiro brought his well-traveled donkey cart right to the veranda so Auntie had very little way to walk. The commander helped her to a seat, then retired to his room behind the shutters.

Everyone on the veranda listened to her stories of Stavros as a little boy, much the same as she would have told if he had truly died. The family cried as if there were an agreed-upon moment. Sophie clung to Auntie like a sesame seed to a honey cake.

All eyes glanced quickly at the shuttered windows and away again, then briefly all around, sharing the secret that Stavros lived on.

They moved their solemn little party into the kitchen, where they might speak more freely. Mama told Auntie she should come to live with them. This had already been decided earlier in the day.

The old woman said the least expected thing. "I'll return to the farm with Spiro." She went on to say Spiro's house was a shambles. His garden untended. He thought of nothing but music and his animals. "Lucky it is for the animals the music doesn't ask to be fed, or they'd starve waiting for the music to finish."

Somehow, she didn't really seem to mind this.

Mama served the evening meal early, a stew of goat's meat and tomatoes over rice. Only when the commander's door opened, and the scrape of his tray was heard by all, and the door closed again, did Uncle Spiro whisper the story of a fine joke that had been played on the Germans.

On a mountain not far from the Needle, where the wind blew without ceasing, a kite made of a Greek flag flew. It could be seen in two villages, and the soldiers felt the insult. When a few of them were sent out to find it, they returned empty-handed.

The next day the kite danced on the air, finally reaching a height where it was merely a dark speck against the blue. A few more soldiers rushed to a distant hillside to capture the kite flyer. They couldn't find him, and the kite still flew. The string was oddly invisible against the sky.

Rifle shots didn't touch the kite. It flew proudly for several days, irritating only those who wore a German uniform.

The villagers worried the kite was growing a little ragged, buffeted about by the winds that blew so strongly at that height. But still it looked good.

Finally the kite broke or was cut loose. But when it might have been expected to fall, the wind snatched it and carried it away. Uncle Spiro smiled at everyone around the table. They understood the joke in this, but who could laugh with the commander next door? Who could cheer?

Listening to this story, Petros pictured Stavros flying the kite. He felt the warmth of sunlight on his shoulders, stood against the wind in his imagination as if it ruffled his own hair, imagined the world spread out below him, the way only someone standing at the top of the Needle could really see it.

Petros met Zola's grin with his own.

Pronunciation Guide

Petros—PEH-trohss

Zola—zoh-LAH

Stavros—STAH-vrohss

Elia—ih-LEE-uh

Panayoti—pa-na-YO-tee

Lambros—LAHM-brohss

Popi—POH-pee

AKILA COULOUMBIS
(1932–2009)

one author's note
(about the other author)

War Games is a true story. It's my husband's story.

Akila was born in Utica, New York, in 1932. His parents had settled in America in the twenties as small-business owners and returned to the farm in Greece when it seemed the only way to weather the Depression. He was six months old then.

In the late thirties, as his parents prepared to come back to the States, war was declared in Europe. England was at war with Germany, and boats traveling between continents were being sunk by German submarines. The family couldn't travel safely.

In 1941, the Germans occupied Greece because they wanted to control the Suez Canal. It was a serious situation for Greek citizens. It got worse fast because the Greek army, returning home to their families, began to do things to hamper the Germans' progress. They cut down the telephone lines, causing many fathers and older boys of a family to be assigned by the Germans to guard the phone lines in front of their homes and farms. If these men and boys were not successful at keeping the Greek army from cutting the lines, their own family members could be, and often were, shot dead.

It was in this scary atmosphere that a high-ranking German officer was installed in Akila's home. Because Akila's father feared for his children, who had dual citizenship, he hadn't followed the edict to register the family with the German authorities as American citizens. But he hadn't anticipated this development. They were an American family living in close quarters with the enemy, their lives endangered until the Germans withdrew in 1944.

Akila and I touched on many other hardships of the occupation: food was scarce, money was worthless, radios and farm implements that could be used as weapons were taken away, people were not allowed to go out of their homes after dark. But Akila remembers most of these events as a time of great adventure.

He grew closer to his family, appreciating his mother's cooking and the security of his father's farm. There was a more exciting element to the usual marble games and kite making and boyish pranks. There was real danger in the true events we've incorporated in this story. But boys being boys, it all seemed part of a larger, meaner game being played by men.

If you were to sit and talk with Akila, he would tell you the stories that make up our chapters actually happened several months apart. We've condensed these events into the early days of the occupation because we thought it would be more enjoyable to read a story that happens all at once.

Also, you'd learn that several commanders lived in his home, one at a time, over the course of the war. One of them guessed the family's secret, but he didn't report them. We like to think he's the commander we're writing about.

We based our main character, Petros, on Akila. Zola is an

idea guy like Akila's brother, Peter, and Akila's sisters are rolled into one girl named Sophie.

Because we set the story when the Germans first arrived, there's a happy ending we didn't tell. In 1945, the Allies won the war and Akila's family returned safely to New York.

Akila and his family in their joint passport photo, when they returned to the United States after the war. From left to right, Akila, Aspasia, Mama Nicky, Peter, Papa Fotti, Minerva. Akila was twelve years old.

acknowledgments

The authors thank Linda Sue Park, who shared childhood stories with Akila at a book fair in Rochester, New York. Both of them went away with story ideas, and for Akila, it was a first encouragement to think of his as a book.

We also thank Richard Peck, who asked Audrey, at a supper with Teri Lesesne, are you going to write his story? And Jesse Perez, who, midway through the chaos, made the difficulties of writing the multisided events of a childhood sound like something that could be smoothed out like a wrinkled map and read with ease. And Y York, who, as we approached the finish line, teased out more story and encouraged us to work just a little harder.

Last but not least, we thank Jenni Holm, who talked childhood stories with Akila while she cooked for us in Hudson, and then said, "Why, that's a story you *have* to write! They all are. Kids would love these stories. You'd start at the kite string, don't you think?" She set us on the road to here.

We started at the kite string, and over several years of working, in between life and other projects, we started several other ways, too, until we had a story line, whittled down to the fewest number of weeks possible, and had used up most of the energy we had for climbing over the remaining stumbling blocks. Which is why we are so grateful to our agent, Jill Grinberg, for seeing the value in this work, and to our editor, Shana Corey, who supported us with her insight and excellent questions through the last labors. Also thanks to our art director, Ellice M. Lee, and our copy editor, Renée Cafiero.

We thank those family members who recalled the reasons why, reminded us of something nearly forgotten, related the story of, debated the details of, knew the fact of or the name of or the how it worked, and just generally jogged the collective memory of a life lived several decades ago in another country. We know this isn't perfectly how it was, but we've done as well as we can with a bigger story told on a smaller scale.

We thank Fotti, Nicky—Akila's parents—and his siblings, Aspasia, Peter, and Minerva. Their memories and contributions made this book possible.

We also thank cousins Fotti, Aspasia, Efthemios, Vivi, George, and Sofia for lively conversations, in person and over the phone. Many thanks to Mema for research. And to Mema and Katingo for an enjoyable afternoon trip through memories and old artifacts, and special thanks to Vasso.

Much love and remembrance to Akila's cousins, and Gerasimos (who is Stavros in our story and who died resisting the occupation), and Zola, and Nicholas Drosos, who spent those cold nights in the well.

about the authors

AUDREY COULOUMBIS's first book for children, *Getting Near to Baby,* won the Newbery Honor in 2000. Audrey is also the author of several other highly acclaimed books for young readers, including *The Misadventures of Maude March,* which was named a Book Sense 76 Pick, a New York Public Library 100 Titles for Reading and Sharing Selection, and a National Parenting Publications Gold Award Winner; and *Love Me Tender,* a Book Sense Children's Summer Pick. She is married to Akila Couloumbis.

AKILA COULOUMBIS was born in New York and spent his childhood in Greece. During World War II, German officers boarded in his family's parlor. This is Akila's first book. Akila and Audrey live in upstate New York and Florida. They have two grown children.